The Hidden Legacy

By

Ellen Dugan

The Hidden Legacy
Copyright @ Ellen Dugan 2017
Edited by Katherine Pace
Copy Editing and Formatting by Libris in CAPS

This is a work of fiction. Names, characters, businesses, organizations, places, events and incidents either are the product of the author's imagination or are used fictitiously. Any resemblance to actual persons, living or dead, events, or locales is entirely coincidental.

No part of this book may be reproduced, or stored in a retrieval system, or transmitted in any other form or by any means electronic, mechanical, photocopying, recording or otherwise without the express written permission of the publisher.

Published by Ellen Dugan

Other titles by Ellen Dugan

THE LEGACY OF MAGICK SERIES

Legacy of Magick, Book # 1

Secret of the Rose, Book # 2

Message of the Crow, Book # 3

Beneath An Ivy Moon, Book # 4

Under The Holly Moon, Book # 5

The Hidden Legacy, Book # 6

Spells Of The Heart, Book # 7

Sugarplums, Spells & Silver Bells, Book # 8

Magick & Magnolias, Book # 9 (Coming 2018)

THE GYPSY CHRONICLES

Gypsy At Heart, Book 1

Gypsy Spirit, Book 2 (Coming 2018)

ACKNOWLEDGMENTS

A special thanks goes to my family, crew of editors, and beta readers.

For the fans of the *Legacy Of Magick* series. As requested, here is Hannah's story as a standalone! I hope you enjoy the little side trip to Massachusetts, meeting another magickal family, and learning about the Osborne and Pogue legacies.

The Posey Ring Charm

For the true of heart, the poesy ring is but a boon,

For all others, the emerald surely spells their doom.

If your lover is untrue, the stone turns a cloudy green,

Should the jewel stay bright and clear, then many blessings will it bring.

To a steadfast soul the legacy passes, heavy though it may be,

To become bewitched and beloved, blessed by the moon, stars, and sea.

-Ellen Dugan

The Hidden Legacy

The human heart has hidden treasures, In secret kept, in silence revealed;

The thoughts, the hopes, the dreams, the pleasures,

Whose charms were broken if revealed.

-Charlotte Bronte

PROLOGUE

"Only the true of heart can hold the ring."

I blinked in surprise at my grandmother, her comment had been out of the blue. Alone in the hospital room with her, I debated whether or not I should call my parents back in or buzz for a nurse. It was a horrible thing to see the woman, who'd been so feisty and tough, brought down to bedridden and frail.

Was the medicine they'd given her earlier causing hallucinations? I wondered. She'd been ill for weeks and the doctors had advised us to say our goodbyes.

"It's okay Grandma," I said, keeping my voice low and soothing. "Don't push yourself. Try and rest." I sat beside her on the bed and laid my hand gently on top of hers.

"I'll have plenty of time to rest, soon enough." Her eyes opened and she focused on me.

"Hi Grandma Oz." I smiled at her.

Janet Osborne's blue eyes were lucid and aware. "Hannah, it will come to you. You're the next in the

Osborne line."

"Sure, okay," I said, trying to soothe her.

"Watch for the pirate," she said. "You'll know him when you see him."

"Do you mean Eli? He dresses like a pirate every day," I reminded her. "Your great-grandson sleeps in his pirate hat."

"I love that little boy," she said of my soon-to-be four year old. "You've done well there."

"He'll be here to visit you this afternoon," I promised, brushing her hair back from her face.

"The pirate, Hannah. Watch for your beloved."

"I will. Absolutely." *Poor thing, they must have whacked her up with some really good drugs,* I thought.

"It's not the drugs. I am *not* hallucinating, I'll have you know," she snapped. Outside the hospital, a storm began to gather.

Thunder rolled and I smiled. "I never said you were."

"No, but you thought it."

"Stay out of my head, Grandma," I said automatically.

She managed to glare at me. "If there was ever a time to be indulgent of an eccentric old Crone, it would be now." Her gown slid off of one shoulder and revealed a faded butterfly tattoo.

I automatically straightened the gown and glanced around to double check that we were still alone. "The Crone is a respected and revered aspect of the triple goddess," I said quietly. "You taught me that."

"You're strong. Always have been," she said. "You use your gifts and intuition well, assisting your friend Edmund with his investigations..."

"I'd like to think so."

"I know so," she said, "and I'm thankful I was here long enough to see you go from Maiden to Mother."

The wind picked up and howled past the window of her room. I tilted my head towards the window and the wind that rattled the glass. "Is that you?" I asked, trying to make her smile.

My grandmother shut her eyes. "I don't have the control over my powers that I used to..."

I focused on the wind screaming outside, and the intensity lessened, and the rattling stopped. "There," I said. "That's better."

"You've come into your own in the past few years. I'm proud of you. I only wish I had longer. I would have liked to see Eli grow up."

I tried to smile. Tried to be brave. "Grandma, don't talk like that."

"You need to pay attention to me now," she insisted, her voice going up.

"Don't get upset," I said. "I'm right here. Do you want me to call Mom back in?" I shifted, planning to go and get my mother.

"Listen to me!" Her hand clamped down on mine. "It won't go to your sister, or your brother," she said. "The legacy *must* be handed down to you."

"What legacy?" I asked, easing back down beside her.

My grandmother coughed a little and I offered her some water. I held the straw to her lips, waited while she sipped. "Better?" I asked.

She nodded her head. "The Osborne legacy," she said, sounding desperate. "It all started with an ancestor named Felicity…and our family kept it hidden and safe for two hundred years. From my grandfather to my father, to me, and then to your mother. She's been holding it these last few months. But now it's your turn. Your duty."

"My turn? My duty to do what?"

"It's your responsibility to hold the jewel now."

"The jewel?"

"The emerald. It's enchanted…bewitched and set in a silver ring," she said, and I felt a jolt go all the way to my toes.

"I've never seen you wear an emerald ring." My mind raced as I considered what she was telling me.

"It's not merely a ring, Hannah. It's our legacy. There's a charm, a spell that was laid upon it over two hundred years ago."

"By whom?" I asked, trying to clarify.

"Felicity," my grandmother insisted as rain began to beat against the windows. "You *must* remember."

"Felicity," I repeated. "I'll remember."

"Mark my words." My grandmother took a careful breath. "The poesy ring, for the true of heart is but a boon," she chanted. "For all others, the emerald surely spells their doom."

The hair rose on the back of my neck. "Go on," I said.

My grandmother's gaze was steady as she linked her hands with mine. "To a steadfast soul the legacy passes, heavy though it may be; to become bewitched and beloved, blessed by the moon, stars, and sea."

The summer storm broke. Lightning flashed and thunder shook the building. The monitors at her bedside began to beep and ring. The shrill sounds had my heart racing. My parents came rushing back into the room, and I heard my father shouting for a nurse.

"Grandma!" I squeezed her hands. "Stay with me!"

"I love you Hannah," she said.

They were the last words she ever spoke.

CHAPTER ONE

I stood in the bright summer sunshine on the high hill that overlooked the harbor of Danversport, Massachusetts, holding my son's hand. It was one month from the day that my grandmother had died, and my family was still adjusting to a world without Grandma Oz in it.

I was still adjusting to it. I thought, and bent down to place a bouquet of daisies on the grave. A yellow butterfly fluttered past and I smiled. My grandmother always had a real affection for butterflies. She'd been an Air Witch, and had surrounded herself with all things associated with that element. From the canaries she had as pets, to the butterfly garden she'd planted for my mother, the bees she'd kept, even the tattoo she'd had on her shoulder.

"Mama?" Eli asked, tugging on my fingers. Today he was wearing a pirate themed t-shirt, denim shorts, and sneakers. His tricorn hat was clutched respectfully over his heart as we stood beside the grave.

"Yes, baby?"

"Is Nana Oz watching over us?"

I smiled, watching as the butterfly flew farther away. "I'm sure she is."

"That's what Pops said." Eli swung our hands back and forth.

I grinned down at him. "Well if Pops says so, it must be true," I agreed, thinking of my father.

"I like seeing the boats!" Eli smiled at me. His first baby tooth had come out the week before. He squinted up at the sun, his pale blonde hair waved in the breeze. His eyes, the same denim blue as mine, were curious as he viewed the old cemetery and out to the port below.

"Is my daddy buried here?" he asked casually.

Caught off guard, I glanced down at him. "No. He's not," I said, trying to answer him as simply as he'd asked.

"He's in 'lington?" Eli struggled to pronounce the word.

"Arlington," I said.

"Cause he was a solider." Eli nodded.

"That's right," I agreed. "He was a soldier." Eli didn't remember his father, he'd only been a baby when John had been killed in action. I ran my hand over Eli's bright sunny hair, shades lighter than mine. The pale blonde tresses my son had inherited from his father.

John had been a good father to Eli for the short time he'd had with him. I sighed, and wondered for the millionth time if I was doing everything right. Being both mother and father to my little boy.

My worrying seemed for nothing, as Eli changed topics in the blink of an eye. He tucked his hat under one arm, pulled his little spy glass out of his back pocket, aimed it at the port below and chattered on about boats, the upcoming fourth of July fireworks, and his all consuming obsession, *pirates.*

"Ready to go, sailor?" I asked him.

"I'm watching the ships, mom," he answered. "The bad guys might be planning to plunder the port."

I rolled my eyes. *I really needed to have a talk with my father about watching old pirate movies with Eli. It was only making the pirate fixation worse.* "That's a good idea," I agreed. "But maybe we should take a walk down at the marina." Eli's head snapped up at my words. "That way you could be sure that we are prepared, in case of an invasion."

"Aye, aye!" He clapped his hat on his head and scrambled for the car.

The drive to the marina was a short one, and I'd barely put the car in park before Eli had unbuckled himself from his booster seat.

"Hang on," I warned him.

I went around the car and opened the door for him. He hopped down, still wearing his hat, grabbed my hand and began tugging me along towards the marina. We walked along the little boardwalk and viewed the boats in dock. There were all sorts of boats here. Pleasure boats, yachts, fishing boats, house boats, sailboats, and cabin cruisers.

Eli beamed as he walked along. I kept his hand in mine, and movement out of the corner of my eye caught my attention. A man stood on the deck of a fancy sailboat, checking the rigging. His dark blonde hair was tousled, curly, and he had a mustache and goatee. He wore long khaki shorts and an unbuttoned blue chambray shirt which framed a strip of very nicely tanned and toned chest.

"Wow," I said under my breath, doing my best not to ogle the eye candy that was a few yards away.

"Mama," Eli breathed. "It's a pirate!" He pointed directly at the same man I was pretending not to stare at.

"Eli." I gave his fingers a light squeeze. "He's just a man working on his boat."

"Nuh-uh." Eli shook his head. "*That's* a pirate."

The man looked up at Eli's words. His sunglasses shielded his eyes, and he flashed a lopsided grin, but it was gone almost as quickly as I'd caught it.

The breeze blew past him and towards me. As it washed over me I picked up on the scent of the harbor, and the tiniest bit of psychic information about the man. *Intelligence, shrewdness, and maybe...destiny.* My stomach flipped.

Eli stood and stared at the man. I tried not to do the same. Instead, I shook off the psychic information, sending a friendly smile in his direction. The man nodded in response. Then he returned his attention to his boat.

I felt a momentary pang at not being striking enough to hold the man's attention, but I shrugged it off, reminding myself to be happy with what I had. Neither short nor tall, I was a curvy five foot seven. My hair tended to misbehave, so I let it grow past my shoulders, and its only redeeming quality was that it was a nice shade of honey blonde. My eyes were a denim blue, nothing exotic, and *nothing* that inspired men to passion.

I was comfortable with my looks, but they were dead average—apparently all the gorgeous genes had gone to my older and younger siblings.

The breeze shifted and the aroma of fried food wafted over me. "How about we go get some lunch, at Mona's?" I tried to distract Eli.

"Can I have chicken fingers?"

"Yes, you can."

"Let's go!" Eli tugged me along to the little dockside lobster shack down from the pier. We walked to a simple building clad in weathered wood faded to silvery-gray. It faced the marina and boasted a smattering of umbrella covered, rustic picnic tables. A huge bright red lobster was painted on the side of the building. *Mona's Lobster Shack* had been around forever, and what it lacked in style, it more than made up for with the food.

The glass window slid open. "What can I get you?" asked the teenager working the front.

After placing our orders, Eli and I sat under the shade of a picnic table umbrella, enjoying the cooler breeze off the water. The seats gave us a great view of the port, and I could also still see that man working on his boat in the distance. *Not that I was interested anyway...I'd learned my lesson about mingling with outsiders. Very few could accept anything beyond what they considered the norm.* The wind toyed with my hair and I tucked a few wayward strands behind my ear.

But still, I tried to remember the last time any guy had made me perk up and notice him. It had been a while. The only men in my life these days was my father, my best friend Edmund, and of course the little one currently wearing a pirate hat and using his toy spyglass to watch the horizon.

"Keep a weather eye…" Eli mumbled to himself.

I grinned at him, snuck my phone out of my purse and took a few pictures of my boy with the marina in the background. *He was so damn cute.* And growing up *so* fast. I tried not to feel sad that in a year, he'd be starting Kindergarten.

"Here you go." Mona Trask, owner and cook of *Mona's Lobster Shack*, dropped off the baskets herself. "Chicken tenders and fries for Eli, and a lobster roll and coleslaw for you."

"French fries!" Eli set his spyglass on the table and pounced on his lunch.

The scent of the lobster roll hit, and my mouth watered. "Thanks, Mona."

"Would you tell your folks I'll be in to pick up my spice order tomorrow before the holiday?"

"Sure," I said, and proceeded to squirt ketchup on the fries for my son.

"Your sister Kayleigh is the only person I trust to mix my spices for my recipes," Mona said.

I smiled. "She'll be happy to hear you say that."

"Seriously," Mona said, "your parents have the best spice shop north of Boston."

They did indeed, I thought. What had started as a tiny little store front when I'd been Eli's age was now a booming local business. My parents specialized in bulk spices, teas and custom blends of spice mixes. "I'll remind Kayleigh and she'll make sure they are ready to go."

"Both the seasoned salt for the fries *and* the spices for the fish batter." Mona reminded me.

"Sure," I said, picking up my phone. "I'll text her now."

"Eat all your food," Mona said to Eli.

"Aye, aye!" Eli said with his mouth full.

"You scalawag." Mona patted his shoulder and went to help her next customers.

Eli slurped his soda through his straw. "Mona makes the best chicken fingers."

I sent my text and raised an eyebrow at him. "Are they better than mine?"

He grinned at me. "Maybe."

I pretended to be offended. "That's a *horrible* thing

to say to your mother." I pressed my hand to my heart for dramatic effect.

"Grandma says that." Eli giggled at me. "She says it *just* like that."

"I know."

"Pop says Grandma is a drama queen."

I swallowed wrong, coughed and thumped my fist against my chest. "You shouldn't repeat that, Eli." If my mother heard that she'd have my father's head on a platter.

"Why?" He frowned up at me. "Grandma's funny, and I like it best when she makes the plants and flowers dance."

I flinched and glanced around, but no one was close enough to overhear us. "What's the family rule, Eli?" I asked.

"Don't talk about mag—"

"Rutabaga," I cut him off, and he started to giggle.

Rutabaga was the family code word for 'magick'. My family had a strict code of silence with outsiders. We kept our Craft quiet and our spiritual beliefs hidden. We always had.

My father had started the 'rutabaga rule' when I'd been little. It had been silly fun for my sister, brother and me, *and* it had helped us to remember not to talk about certain things with mundanes. Now my older sister and I were both trying to teach the 'To be silent' rule to our own children.

But in a world where Hogwarts and boy wizards

were a part of popular culture, it was harder than ever for our kids to remember, and to stick to the rules.

"I like it when she makes the ru-bagel," Eli said.

Ru-bagel, I struggled to keep a solemn expression on my face as his mangling of the word. *That was his best one yet.*

I sat there studying my little boy with ketchup smeared on his mouth and his tricorn hat on his head. He flashed me an angelic smile, and I couldn't help but grin. "Eli?" I said.

"Yeah?" he answered with a mouth full.

"I love your face," I told him.

My phone chimed, signaling a text message. I flipped the phone over from where I'd set it on the table. It was from my mother.

I'd like to speak to you. When will you be home?

"Who's that?" Eli wanted to know.

"It's your grandma," I answered.

"Can I send a smiley face?"

"Sure," I said. "Gimme a second." I typed in a quick answer.

Be home in a half hour.

I handed the phone to Eli who competently chose a smiley emoji, spelled out his name, and hit send.

My mother responded with a few kissy face emojis, and I tucked the phone away.

Eli plowed through his lunch and I finished my lobster roll. I looked out over the marina and tried not to be too disappointed that the eye candy on the sailboat was no longer in my view.

***

Eli and I strolled past the family herb garden and climbed the stairs to our little apartment that was on the second floor of the detached double garage on my parent's property. We'd moved in when Eli had been six months old and his father had been killed in action.

The arrangement worked for us, as it gave me some privacy, and my parents were close by...as in across the driveway close by. The garage below our apartment was now my workshop where I created, painted and stenciled seasonal themed wooden signs for my parent's store, and for my online shop.

The apartment wasn't large, but we didn't need much. A combination living room and kitchen, a bathroom, and two small bedrooms. I had decorated it simply. It was bright and airy, and I'd managed to make sturdy blue denim slipcovers for my second hand couch, throw pillows and even curtains for my home.

I unlocked the door and Eli rushed in ahead of me. Our cat, Sam, sat in the kitchen window, and he gave a loud meow in greeting. The cat watched suspiciously as Eli ran to his room with a battle cry.

Eli was out seconds later brandishing his plastic sword and having a duel with his imaginary friend Captain Time. So intent on his battle, he whacked against the large, wooden 'Fresh Honey' sign that hung in the living room. The sturdy sign didn't even shift. I'd made it myself. It had a vintage distressed finish and was golden-yellow, with deep navy stenciling that featured a large honeybee.

"Be careful with the sword," I said automatically.

"No quarter given!" Eli bellowed, hacking away at the air.

"Where'd you learn *that*?" I asked him.

Eli stopped. "Captain Time taught me."

I kept my expression neutral. "Well then, you and the Captain should take this battle into your room, Grandma is coming over."

Eli swept his hat off his head and made a sort of bow. "Yes, m'lady," and he strolled into his room.

I shook my head at his retreating back. I'd assumed that Eli's pirate obsession had simply been a phase, but now I was starting to get a little concerned. *M'lady? No quarter given?*

A knock sounded a second before the door opened. "Hello?" my mother called out, poking her head in the door.

"Hey Mom." I motioned her in, and was surprised to see my father with her. Maryanne and Padrick Pogue strolled in, holding hands. My mom had the same honey blonde hair as I, but she had bangs and added highlights. My father's hairline was receding, and his blonde hair and neatly trimmed beard were almost all gray now. He was too thin and trim to ever pass for Santa Claus, but the long ZZ Top style beard made many of the local children gaze at him with large eyes every December.

The fact that my parents still held hands like teenagers after thirty five years of marriage gave me hope that someday I'd find a love like that.

"You." I pointed accusingly at my father. "No more pirate movies, or Renaissance Faires. Eli's pirate fascination is getting a little extreme."

"Aw, he's just a boy. Let him play." My father shrugged away my concerns and tucked his hands in the pockets of his jeans.

"Ever since you bought that tricorn hat for Eli he's refused to take it off," I said.

My father's response was a quick grin.

"I told you not to buy that," my mother said, and playfully smacked his shoulder.

"Dad, did you two hang out with a bunch of pirate players at the Ren Faire last month?" I wanted to know.

"No we didn't, and Eli was disappointed we missed the Pirate Weekend."

"Well, I suppose I should be thankful for small favors. Because you should hear some of the stuff he's been saying lately."

"Padrick," my mother began, "why don't you take Eli outside and keep him busy while Hannah and I have a little chat."

"Sure." My father dropped a kiss on my mother's mouth and began to stomp loudly across the apartment, calling for Eli. He slammed the bedroom door open and mock growled at Eli. "Surrender or die!"

"By the goddess." My mother rolled her eyes to the ceiling as the battle cries of grandfather and grandson filled the apartment. "And he accuses *me* of being dramatic."

And sure enough, after a bit of a chase and grab, my father was carting out my son, upside down, by one leg, as if he'd taken a hostage. "We're going outside," my father said around the plastic sword that was clamped between his teeth.

"Dad!" I tossed up my hands. "This is *not* helping!"

"Damn your eyes!" Eli shouted.

"Eli! Watch your language!" I said, while my mother gaped at the cursing from a four year old, and my father began to laugh.

A few seconds later, my father and his captive disappeared. I could hear them going down the steps, I moved to an open window and glanced out. There they were, playing sword fight on the backyard grass, with the butterfly and herb gardens behind them.

My mother joined me and we stood watching them. As usual, she smelled of herbs and the garden. She was a talented magickal herbalist, a skill that she'd passed onto my sister, and one that came in very handy running the spice shop.

"He's as bad as Eli." I cringed when Eli nailed my father in the back of the leg with his plastic sword.

"*That's* going to leave a mark," my mother said.

I snorted out a laugh. "So what did you want to talk

to me about?"

My mother's eyes slid from the scene outside to my face. "I came to talk to you about your inheritance. About the Osborne legacy."

CHAPTER TWO

My mother went to the kitchen table. "Come and sit," she invited.

I took the chair opposite of her, and even though my heart was racing, I casually folded my hands on the table top.

"You know that the lawyers read the will a few days ago," my mother said. "Your Uncle Robert and I had to go through all of Grandma's things so we could pass along the personal items she had set aside for each of her children and grandchildren."

My heart broke a little for my mother. "I'm sorry, that couldn't have been easy."

"Robert took charge of the family papers, for his research on the family tree," my mother said.

"Well, that makes sense." I nodded. "That's always been his thing. He loves genealogy."

She smiled. "I divided up your grandmother's jewelry between you, your sister, and your cousin Rowan. The butterfly locket, earrings and bracelet specifically. She would want you girls to each have one of her butterfly theme pieces."

"That would be nice. I'd like to have one."

"Also there is some money for both you and Eli, and then there's this." My mother pulled a small wooden box out of her purse and placed it in the middle of the table. "Your inheritance."

The box was maybe three inches square and was elaborately carved with a butterfly on the lid. Seeing it had my heart jumping. "Is this about what grandma told me the day she passed away?"

"Yes," my mother said, watching me carefully.

"I remember when I shared with you and dad what she'd said to me right before she died, you weren't surprised by it."

"No," she said. "We weren't"

She rested her fingertips on the box. "This has been in my care for the past few months, ever since your grandmother began to decline. I've been a temporary guardian, of sorts, but this was always meant for you."

"It was?"

"When you were born, your grandmother foresaw that it would be your duty."

"Duty," I repeated, thinking back to what Grandma had told me. "But why mine?" I asked. "Why not *your* duty. You were her only daughter. Or why not Kayleigh? She's the oldest."

My mother brushed at her bangs. "Your grandmother insisted that it would be you. Not Kayleigh, not Nathan, but *you*." She smiled. "It was one of the reasons your middle name is Osborne."

My eyes flashed to hers. "When Eli was born she insisted his middle name should be Osborne, too." I shook my head. "Here I thought she'd been upset because his father and I never married."

"Hardly." Mom laughed. "She *never* legally married your grandfather either, and insisted on keeping her maiden name—which she passed onto my brother and I."

"She was a woman ahead of her time," I said with a grin.

"That she was," Mom sighed. "But they had fifty years together, and I've never seen such a strong bond as my parents shared."

"I have," I said. "The love you and dad share makes me hope for something like that for myself someday."

My mother reached across the table and squeezed my hand. "Bottom line, Hannah, she wanted to be sure that the Osborne name was handed down."

"Uncle Robert has three kids—two of them boys," I pointed out. "If this is an 'Osborne lineage thing' then she should have passed it on to Uncle Robert and his children."

"You're missing the point." Her voice rose with her frustration. "This legacy is meant to be passed on to the individual who is *worthy* to hold it. It has been passed down over the centuries—to both sons and daughters...but *always* to an Osborne."

I frowned. "Okay. If you say so."

"Hannah, do you remember everything your grandmother told you, that last day?"

I sat back in my chair. "She told me that the Osborne legacy, started with Felicity…and that our family magick had kept it hidden and safe for two hundred years. That it was my turn now, and my duty."

"And?" she prompted.

"She told me to keep watch for a pirate, but maybe that was from the medication they had her on."

"What else did she say?" My mother's blue eyes watched me carefully.

"Grandma spoke about a bewitched jewel and a poesy ring."

My mother nodded, reached out and flipped up the lid on the hinged box. "This is the poesy ring that first belonged to Felicity."

I felt my eyes grow wide. The old ring was nestled inside of its carved box. The band was silver and heavy. I could see words carved inside of the band. But it was the jewel set in the ring that was the most impressive. The emerald caught the light coming through the kitchen window and seemed to pulse. A glowing shade of grass-green with blue undertones. "Good gods!" I breathed.

My mother chuckled. "When my mother first showed me the ring, and explained about our legacy, you were an infant, and I had pretty much the same reaction."

"That's got to be worth a fortune!"

"I did some internet sleuthing," Mom said.

"You did?"

"You're not the only one with a nose for investigations." My mother grinned. "I've paid attention when you talk about your job."

"So what did you discover?"

"The emerald is an oval cabochon, at least five carats." My mother rattled off the amount she estimated the stone to be worth, and had my eyes popping.

"By the goddess." I shook my head. "This should be locked up in a vault somewhere."

"Family history states that the jewel is much older than the ring," Mom said. "That the emerald came from the jungles of South America and was stolen from the Incas by the Spaniards. Next the jewel ended up in the treasure chest of...a *pirate*." She seemed to savor the last word.

I met my mother's eyes. "Really, a pirate?"

She pressed a hand to her throat, as if offended. "Do I look like I'm joking?" Her expression was as serious as I'd ever witnessed.

"No, I can see that you're not," I said, pulling the box a little closer. "From a pirate's treasure, eh?" I shook my head. "Figures."

"Did it ever occur to you that perhaps Eli's fascination with pirates goes deeper than you imagined?"

"Meaning what?" I asked, feeling a chill roll down

my spine.

"Felicity married a sea captain named Christopher Timmons." My mother stared at me. "Captain Timmons. Captain *Time*? Does that sound familiar?"

"You think Eli's imaginary friend is what...a ghost?"

"Not necessarily. Perhaps Eli is simply having past life memories." My mother shrugged.

"Well, ghost or memory, that would help explain the vocabulary." I pulled my fingers away from the carved box, because this was all making me a little anxious. "So I inherited a haunted ring?"

"Hannah, it's more than that. It's a part of our legacy. There's a charm, a spell that was laid upon it over two hundred years ago." She reached inside of her voluminous purse and pulled out an old piece of yellowish paper that was protected in a clear plastic cover. "Your grandmother gave me this too," she said. "You need to see it for yourself."

I took the page and studied it. The writing was still easy to make out. "It doesn't seem very old. Not as old as the ring, anyway."

"Read it," my mother invited. "Out loud."

I cleared my throat, and the sun went behind the clouds. The little beam of sunlight that had illuminated the table disappeared. "*The poesy ring, for the true of heart is but a boon, for all others, the emerald surely spells their doom. If your lover is untrue, the stone turns to a cloudy green, should the jewel stay bright and clear, then many blessings will it bring. To a steadfast soul the legacy passes, heavy though it may be, to become bewitched and beloved, blessed by the moon, stars, and sea."*

"What do you think?" my mother asked.

"Grandma Oz told me most of this, the day she died," I said, setting the page down on the table. "I'm not sure how much of this I buy into."

"Hannah, you were raised understanding magick. Its joys and its burdens." My mother covered my hand with hers. "I am a little surprised, sweetheart, that you find this so hard to accept."

"So now that it's mine what am I supposed to do with it? I obviously can't wear it in public."

"Our practical Hannah." My mother rolled her eyes. "Clearly, you can't wear it in public. However it must stay within your possession."

"Meaning what?"

"Meaning close by you."

"You want me to stash *that* in my sock drawer?' I gaped at her. "What if someone broke in? What if it was stolen? What if Eli found it and—"

"What if purple elephants fall from the sky?"

Her snarky comeback made me laugh. "Good point."

"Sweetheart, I know you've always yearned for adventure and a great love of your own."

I studied my mother from across the table. "Is it that obvious?"

"To me and to your father, yes it is." She sighed. "You've always been so smart, brave and sensible.

Maybe it's time my girl, to let your Irish out and go a little wild."

I laughed. "I can't believe you said that to me."

"Why?" her eyebrows disappeared under her bangs. "You deserve love, happiness and fun as much as anyone else."

Unable to sit, I went to the window. "I need some air," I said, raising the sash. The screen was missing on the kitchen window and I'd not gotten around to having it replaced. Fresh air rushed in and the blue gingham curtains danced in the breeze. I ran my finger along the edge of one fabric panel, reminiscing. Grandma Oz had been with me when I'd found the fabric for the kitchen curtains, and she'd also been the one who'd taught me to sew. "What do I do now?" I wondered.

"For now, keep it close." My mother sat back in her chair. "The ring will reveal its magick to you in time. At least that's what Grandma told me to tell you."

"So this was a blessing to Grandma and Grandpa." I considered that. "I guess the stone must have stayed clear while they were together."

"I'd say so."

"And if you screw up or are unworthy the emerald will curse you instead of bless you?" I ran a hand through my hair. "Well, I guess it's a good thing I'm single."

"According to your grandmother, the ring has a knack for showing you who your future love will be. So if you ever meet someone special, the ring…"

"Would let me know if he's *the* one." I blew out a long breath. "Do you think that's true, Mom?"

"Yes, I believe that it is. All in all, I think you are taking things marvelously well," she said. "If it had been your sister the ring was handed down to—she'd have been positively swooning over the idea of guarding such a family artifact."

"Yeah, and if it had gone to Nathan he'd have gone total archaeology nerd, and would have it on display at a museum." I rolled my eyes thinking of my younger brother who was in Missouri working on his Masters Degree at William's Ford University. "Well." I smiled at her from over my shoulder. "Seems like I'm going to have a little adventure whether I like it or not."

"Don't be afraid of this, Hannah."

"I'm not afraid," I argued. "Only cautious, and I'll admit it, a little curious."

"You use your gifts to solve mysteries and crimes every day," she said. "It only makes sense that you are the current keeper of the legacy." My mother crossed her arms, pleased with her own conclusions.

"Mom, you're making it sound like a television show. I don't *solve* crimes. I run the office and occasionally consult with Edmund on his investigations, *if* he asks for my help."

I noticed movement out of the corner of my eye. A large black and yellow butterfly had flown in through the open window. It circled my head once, fluttered over, and landed on the lid of the carved box.

My mother gasped, and pressed her hands to her lips. "Do you still doubt the ring was meant for you?"

I stared at the Black Swallowtail butterfly. Tears welled up, and my throat felt tight.

"That's a sign. You know it is," she insisted. "Your grandmother found a way to make contact with us."

I held out my hand, and the butterfly fluttered over and landed on my outstretched fingers. "Hi, Grandma Oz," I whispered.

The butterfly flapped its wings once and sailed straight out through the open window. "Blessed be," my mother whispered.

***

A hidden legacy and priceless emeralds aside, I still had a preschooler to wrangle, laundry to do, dinner to fix, and then I had to scrub my son and toss him into bed. I ended up stashing the box in my nightstand drawer under a few pairs of underwear, and a box of condoms that—tragically—hadn't ever seen any use. I added a layer of protection to the ring's hiding place by casting a concealment spell my father had taught me.

Still, knowing the heirloom was in my house made me a little nervous.

Eli hadn't gone to bed without a fight. He was overly wound up from the day and the mock-battle with my father. The typical bedtime routine of bath, book and bed hadn't worked that well, and he'd been pouting when I closed his door with a stern warning of what would happen if he didn't stay in bed.

I folded a few loads of laundry and tried to watch some television, but my mind kept circling back to the carved box in my room. I put away the freshly folded bath towels, and then I held my breath and crept into Eli's room to see if he'd finally fallen asleep.

The night light illuminated the blue walls. My baby boy lay sprawled flat on his back, his arms over his head with his tricorn hat over his face. I crept in and carefully lifted the hat off. I set it on his dresser and snuck out as carefully as I'd gone in. I didn't breathe again until after I'd shut his door.

A short time later I'd washed my face, tossed on a nightshirt and headed off to bed myself. Sam the cat followed me into my room and made himself at home on the blue quilt spread over the white painted wrought-iron bed.

Knowing this might be my only chance at alone time, I shut my door and sat cross-legged in the middle of my bed. I carefully pulled the carved box out of the nightstand and set it in my lap. I opened the lid, took a deep breath and picked up the ring by my fingertips. "It's heavier than I thought." I said to Sam, who ignored me. I set the ring in the center of my palm, waited to see if anything would happen, and was a little disappointed when it sat quietly.

I held up the ring to the light and read the inscription. I tried to sound it out. "*Cuirle mo croide.*" I frowned over the Gaelic words, made a mental note to do some research and translate it. The emerald glowed in the soft light, and unable to resist, I tried it on. As soon as the ring dropped heavily into place, the emerald seemed to pulse with a brighter green light, and to my surprise, my surroundings began to completely fall away.

I didn't fight it. Instead I tucked my thumb over the back of the poesy ring, closed my fingers in a fist, rolled back on my pillows and let the vision crash over me...

I was still in my bedroom, but everything was different. The light was misty, the sound was muffled and the air was heavy and expectant. In the vision, I felt a pair of strong muscular arms wrap around me from behind. I was held firmly but gently, and there was no fear. Instead I felt desire, passion, and excitement.

A man's mouth dropped kisses in the spot between my shoulder and neck. I felt whiskers rub across my skin and I shivered. I didn't recognize the voice that murmured in my ear, but what he said had my heart racing and my muscles quivering in anticipation.

"*Yes*." I heard myself whisper.

In the vision I tried to see his face, but he was wrapped so tightly around me that I couldn't turn my head far enough. He pressed up against my naked skin, and I felt a moment of fear at the sheer size of him.

My head was pulled gently back as he arranged me to his liking. I was held in place by one of his hands on my hip, and the other that was tangled in my hair. He slid in deep and I moaned. My hands gripped the familiar quilt on the bed, and the emerald on my finger seemed to glow in a bright, clear grassy green.

My lover wrapped his arms across my breasts, and pulled me up so that my back was tight against his chest. He was filling me up with long, sure strokes that had me shuddering with pleasure. *He* set the pace and the tone of our lovemaking...slowly and deliberately at first, and then faster and stronger.

I was close. So close to the orgasm of my life. I felt it build and build, and tried one last time to see his face...

The next thing I knew I was sprawled flat on my belly. My head hung off the side of my own bed, and I was staring at the braided blue and yellow area rug on the bedroom floor. I shook my head, and pushed up slowly to my elbows.

"What in the world?" I sat up, patted my chest to make sure I was still clothed, and breathed a sigh of relief when I found that I was in my pajamas. I glanced around the room and reassured myself that I was indeed alone, except for the cat who was sleeping at the foot of the bed. I flopped over to my back against all of the pillows I'd sewn from old scraps of yellow and white quilts, and held up my hand to regard the emerald ring.

I'd never experienced a vision like that, I thought. *One that was so vivid...with so much texture, sensation...and damned if it hadn't seemed real!*

I tried to level my breathing, but my body still throbbed and ached from coming so close to that truly epic orgasm—only to have it suddenly interrupted. I ran my hands down and was slightly embarrassed to discover that my panties were damp from my own arousal. I shifted, uncomfortable, on edge, and tried to recall details from the vision.

I had recognized my own room. The yellow painted dresser, my blue and white quilt...When I closed my eyes and tried to focus on any specifics about the man in the vision, it only made me more needy. I tried to recall exactly what he'd whispered in my ear, and to my shock, an orgasm hit me like a freight train.

"Holy shit," I laughed, panting as the climax ended.

Not sure whether I was delighted or embarrassed by what had happened, I lay there for a moment and caught my breath. Eventually I rolled out of bed, picked up the carved box and set it on my nightstand. I calmly folded back the sheets, hit the lights, and climbed into bed.

After my eyes adjusted to the light of the waxing moon that spilled into my darkened room, I lifted my hand and studied the jewel carefully. *The vision had to be of the future, because I hadn't had a lover in years...or one who'd ever given me that much pleasure.*

"The problem is," I decided, "I have no idea what that future lover even looks like."

Sam walked up me and leaned into my face. "Then

again, Sam, that might be for the best." I patted the cat's head absently. "Knowing too much about your own future can cause all sorts of problems."

The cat didn't have anything to add to my monologue, instead he made himself at home on my chest while I mulled it over. *Well, the ring was certainly living up to its reputation...and wouldn't it be something if I ended up having a sexy little adventure? Me, Hannah Osborne Pogue. Single mother, and all around practical Witch.*

I fell asleep still wearing the poesy ring, smiling over the possibilities.

CHAPTER THREE

The next morning I woke to a bright sunny day, and was more relaxed than I'd felt in weeks. When I remembered why, it made me chuckle. I hopped out of bed, secured the poesy ring back in its carved box, charmed it into concealment again, and headed for the showers.

I dropped Eli off to spend the day with my dad and drove straight to the office. The two story building was directly across the street from my parent's spice shop on Maple Street. *Fox Investigations* had been in business for six years—and I'd been my best friend Edmund's assistant for five of them. Edmund Fox and I had grown up together, our families were close friends, and while he wasn't a magickal practitioner, his mother *was*.

I'd started out as a part-time clerk when I'd been pregnant with Eli, answering phones, filing and doing some computer work. As time had gone by, I'd begun to consult with Edmund on his cases using my particular witchy talents. I had a nose for the truth and for lies, and as my friend had discovered, my clairolfaction abilities came in very, very, handy in his line of work.

For five years it had been only Edmund and me, but that was about to change. Good news? Business was booming, I was now full-time and he was expanding. Bad news? Edmund had recently decided to take on a partner. All I knew of the partner was, he was an old college friend of Edmund's, and that he used to be a cop. I still hadn't found out why his friend was no longer on the force. I was currently debating on whether or not running a background check on the new partner would be ethical.

I unlocked the door, disengaged the security system and went directly to my desk in the front office. I tucked my purse away, turned up the air conditioning, and headed for the back. Above me, I could hear Edmund in his apartment, and a few minutes later he was bounding down the back stairs and into the kitchenette.

"Morning handsome," I called out.

"Morning gorgeous." He skidded to a halt in front of his coffee maker. "You look nice today. Is that a new dress?"

I glanced down at my sky blue, knee-length summer dress. "It is. I got it online for a great price." I answered. The dress was swingy with the cold shoulder style.

"You found that dress online?" His dark eyes grew

wide. "That's fabulous, Hannah. I don't know how you always find such great stuff on sale."

"Thanks, Edmund." I smiled. I needed to be thrifty, as every extra dime I had either went into my craft business or into a savings account for the home I hoped to buy in the future. "You look pretty sharp yourself, too."

My friend leaned against the counter as the machine gurgled out a cup of coffee. He was gym toned, drop dead gorgeous with dark hair and eyes, and impeccably dressed.

"Well, it's not everyday you expand your business, and take on a new partner," he said.

I made a face. "Yeah, don't remind me."

"Jealous, darling?" Edmund teased.

"No, I've never even met your friend," I said, walking over to brew a cup of tea for myself.

I loved my job working with Edmund. But there was no way I could ever reveal my talents in front of an outsider. More importantly, I couldn't imagine an ex-cop being comfortable working with a Witch. Even *if* he actually believed in them.

"We're lucky to have him join us here," Edmund confided.

"How's that?" I asked, popping a K-cup of English Breakfast into the machine.

"Henry Walker had an exemplary career as a homicide detective in Atlanta."

"Had?" I frowned. "Why'd he leave the force in

Atlanta?" I wanted to know.

Edmund paused and seemed to choose his words carefully. "It's not that complicated, Hannah. He decided he wanted a quieter life."

I waited until the cup filled, and thought about what Edmund had said. "Well, he'll get that lifestyle here." I shrugged.

"But?" Edmund asked patiently.

"I think it's wonderful that business is booming, but I'm still not sure how I feel about an outsider coming into our work environment. What if he *notices*?"

"Henry and I were roommates in college. He already knows I'm gay."

I snorted out a laugh, and reached for the milk we kept in the mini-fridge on the back counter. "No, I *meant* what if he notices about me? And my...abilities?"

Edmund's eyes went comically large. "I thought I told you to hide the cauldron!"

"Want some hemlock for that coffee?" I asked deadpan.

He took the carton of milk away from me. "Don't poison me, I'm about to give you a raise."

"You know better than anyone that some people don't react well to anything they consider different." I took the milk back, added some to my tea.

"If you're truly concerned we can always reinstate the rutabaga rule here in the office." Edmund slung an arm around my shoulder and I leaned into him.

"See, this is why I love you." I smiled. "You get me,

my family, and the rules we live by."

"My mother also raised my sister and me to be discreet." Edmund sipped his coffee. "I may not have the gifts you do, but don't worry, Hannah. I have a feeling...Henry Walker being here is going to be a good thing. For all of us."

We settled into our morning routine and Edmund brought me up to speed on the latest town gossip. My friend knew everybody in Danvers, between the investigations and his innate curiosity, he had the inside scoop on practically everyone and everything. From the oldest of the founding families, from all the way back to the Witch trials...to the newcomers.

Shortly before lunchtime, Edmund escorted our oldest client, Mrs. Endicott, to the door. She was in her mid-eighties, the president of her neighborhood homeowner's association, and was typically in once every few weeks to report something to Edmund. A few weeks ago it had been to report that someone or *something* had snitched a few prize roses from her gardens.

To his credit, my friend handled her with a graciousness that I couldn't have managed. When she finally left, I smiled and let out a relieved breath as Edmund closed the door behind her. The old woman always smelled of mothballs, and I was relieved when she left.

"That's one mean old bat," I said as she walked further down the street.

"That she is," he agreed. "But today she became a client."

"You're kidding."

"Nope." He pulled a check out of his pocket. "There were a couple of robberies on her street last week. One of the families were home when the thieves broke in. Scared them pretty badly."

"The Marshalls?" I asked, thinking back.

"Yeah, and Mrs. Endicott is convinced that she's next." He handed me the check. "We've just been hired to investigate the robberies and neighborhood vandalism by the Oak Hills Homeowners Association."

"My sister and her family live in that neighborhood," I said, reaching for the check. When I saw the retainer fee, I jolted in surprise. "Wow, they aren't kidding."

"No they aren't."

I tucked the check away in the lock box, and Edmund returned to his office. I'd only started going through my files when an intriguing scent wafted over me. The a/c unit in the building was new, and I was intrigued to catch the barest hint of the port and the docks.

We were several blocks away from the marina and inside the building, so there was no physical way for the scent to make its way indoors...however, I tended to pick up on fragrances and they often had very specific meanings for me. This one whispered of: *Travel, change, and a journey...*

I snapped my head up. A man stood on the sidewalk,

considering our front windows. He was tall, with tousled dark blonde hair. He squinted against the sun and took his time studying the building. Eventually he reached for the door and walked in.

"May I help you?" I asked.

The man had a neatly trimmed mustache and goatee. He wore khaki slacks and a button down chambray shirt —both could have used a bit of ironing. "Hello," he said, with a slow Southern drawl. "I'm here to see Edmund Fox."

Why did he seem so familiar? I wondered. As I sat there gaping at him, an intense feeling of déjà vu swept over me. *This was the man I'd seen on the docks. The sexy one working on his sailboat...who Eli had decided was a pirate.*

"Henry!" Edmund's happy voice from behind made me practically jump out of my chair. Edmund walked forward all beaming smiles and gave Henry an enthusiastic hug. Henry gave him an awkward pat on the back in return.

Seeing him this close I realized, despite his impressive physical appearance, this man was tired, and *burned out*, if my instincts were correct.

The man smiled slightly and his eyes crinkled at the corners. "Edmund, it's good to see you."

"How was the trip up?" Edmund asked cheerfully.

"Fine." Henry nodded.

"Did you bring your things?" my friend asked.

"I did, it's not much."

Edmund shifted with his arm still around his friend. "Henry, meet Hannah Pogue. She's the other half of *Fox Investigations*. Hannah, this is Henry Walker."

"Hello," I said as he gave me a nod.

"Nice to meet you." His voice was smoky, deep and gravelly.

"Actually, I think we've met before." I heard myself say.

"You have?" Edmund glanced from Henry and back to me.

"At the marina yesterday," I explained and focused on Henry. "You own a sailboat, right?"

He frowned as he thought back. "You were with the kid dressed as a pirate."

"My son, Eli," I said, and tried not to react when he glanced down at my left hand, noted the lack of a wedding band, and gave me a considering stare.

Edmund began talking about paperwork for the new partnership and he nudged Henry back to his office.

My heart sank as they closed the door behind them. Unlike Edmund, I had a *bad* feeling about this. This was the super cop we were lucky to have? He might be attractive but he also struck me as suspicious and judgmental. Not to mention unkempt and slightly sloppy.

What by the moon and stars could my sophisticated and polished friend, and the guy who looked like he rolled out of bed and had showed up to his meeting in the clothes he'd slept in—possibly have in common?

***

After lunch, Henry and Edmund left the building. Edmund had said they were off to get Henry settled, and I was relieved when they were gone for the day. Again, I debated on doing an internet search on Henry Walker. *After all I now knew he'd been a homicide detective in Atlanta.* But by the end of the day, I still hadn't. I was locking the door and preparing to leave when I bumped solidly into him.

"Oh, sorry," I said, and then frowned when he yanked away from me like I'd burned him.

He was carrying a duffle bag, and his face was set. "Edmund told me to pick up the keys for the other apartment from you."

"Certainly," I said stiffly, and turned the keys again so I could unlock the door.

"I didn't figure you were closing early." His tone was accusatory, and put my back up. He followed me in and stopped in the center of the room.

"It's not *early*," I said, going straight to my desk. I pulled the little key chain out for the second apartment upstairs. "It was Edmund who decided to close up at four because of the holiday weekend."

He held out his hand for the keys. "Well, darlin'?" he said impatiently.

"My name is Hannah Pogue," I said through my teeth. "You may call me Hannah, or Ms. Pogue. But *don't* call me darling."

One side of his mouth kicked up. "Sure thing, honey."

I stayed at my desk, held the keys and considered my words carefully. "Mr. Walker, are we going to have a problem working together?"

His eyes were a sizzling bottle-green, but his expression was bland. "Nope. Edmund tells me you're a hell of an office manager and that you've consulted with him on cases."

"I have," I said.

"I don't work with civilian consultants," he announced. "As far as I'm concerned, if you just file and answer the phones darlin'...we'll get along fine."

Bristling at the rude words and condescending tone, I sucked in a breath and was about to let him have it, when Edmund walked in.

"Did you get your keys?" he asked Henry.

"Not yet," Henry said.

I shut the drawer and walked past Henry, and passed the keys to Edmund instead. "You may want to have a few words with your new partner, regarding my position here," I said between my teeth.

"Hannah?" Edmund reached out. "What's the matter?"

Not trusting my temper, I walked past my best friend and went out the door and straight to my car.

I drove home, angry at myself for letting a complete stranger affect me so. I parked my car and started to walk towards the back patio of my parent's home. I'd managed about two steps forward when their backdoor opened.

I stared at the stunning young man who stepped onto the back patio. He brushed his hair away from his face, met my eyes and grinned. "Hey, Sis."

Bad mood forgotten, my jaw dropped as I recognized my brother. "Nathan?"

"Surprise." He grinned.

I squealed and ran straight at him. "Holy crap! You're here!" I jumped into my little brother's arms.

He caught me. "You look good, Hannah."

I eased back and laughed. "Good grief, you're still gorgeous. How are you? How long are you staying?"

"For about a week."

"So you're here through the fourth?" I hugged him again and saw movement over his shoulder. A young woman stood in the doorway. "Hello," I said cautiously.

She was dressed in a black tank top, ripped denim shorts and black trainers. Her hair was a rich brown and cut in a long bob. The green eyes that studied us were outlined with smoky eye shadow, and struck me as friendly and curious.

"You going to introduce us, Pogue?" She raised an eyebrow at my brother, and leaned a shoulder against the doorframe. Two silver pendants hung around her neck, a crescent moon, a large pentagram, and also a fancy digital camera.

Nathan tucked an arm around my shoulder. "Ivy this

is my sister, Hannah. Hannah meet my girlfriend, Ivy Bishop."

I stuck out a hand. "It's nice to meet you." Nathan had talked to me about Ivy. But it still made me blink seeing the gothic and very openly practicing Witch paired up with my quiet and serious younger brother.

Ivy pushed away from the door, ignored my outstretched hand, and gave me a quick hug in greeting. She released me, her eyes traveling from Nathan and back to me. "Yeah, I can see some family resemblance."

The air shifted around us, and even with the brief embrace I detected the fragrance of cherries and chocolate, and very happy vibrations radiating from her. I also picked up on a *lot* of personal power. "Nice to meet you," I said, and meant it.

"I'd like to photograph you sometime." Ivy tipped her head as if considering.

"Run, Hannah," Nathan said. "I'll cover you."

I chuckled. "You should photograph him instead. He's prettier than me."

"I already did." Ivy grinned. That's how I met him, taking his picture on campus."

I glanced at my brother. "I bet *that* went over well."

Eli slammed out the back door, plastic sword in hand, wearing his tri-corn hat as usual. "Mom! Uncle Nathan is home!" He ran towards us and threw himself at my brother.

Nathan scooped Eli up and settled him on his hip. I grinned over at my brother and son and heard the click of a camera.

"Gotcha." Ivy stepped back and framed in another shot

Eli laughed and grinned at the camera. "Take my picture, Ivy!"

Ivy began to circle the three of us. Her camera clicked away, and I realized as I watched her that photography wasn't merely a hobby for Ivy Bishop.

I tried to duck out of the picture taking session, but Nathan kept me clamped at his side. Eventually I ignored the camera and instead smiled at my brother and son.

***

With my brother's surprise visit, we ended up having a barbeque that night. While my dad grilled turkey burgers and ears of corn on his fancy gas grill, I was pressed into helping my mother set up additional tables so the entire family could eat outside together in the shade of the covered patio. Mom rushed back inside to finish a salad, and I snapped out a few checkered tablecloths and set the tables with my mother's casual melamine plates.

My older sister Kayleigh sat in a padded chair nursing her baby, while her five year old daughter Margot ran around the back yard, chasing Eli.

Dad and my brother-in-law Curtis were discussing sports, while Nathan and Ivy hauled out folding chairs.

When the chairs were in place Nathan went and sat with Kayleigh so he could meet his new niece, and I found myself alone with Ivy Bishop.

Not sure what to make of her, I stuck to safe topics. "So, Nathan tells me you two are off to Salem day after tomorrow?"

Ivy grabbed the cutlery and started to add knives and forks to the plates. "Yeah, I can't wait," she said. "I want to see all the touristy things, and visit the Witch Trials Memorial."

"Be sure and visit the graveyard. It's the second oldest in the country." I said, working my way along the tables.

Once we finished setting the tables, Ivy looped her arm in mine. "Give me a little tour, Hannah." She gave me a friendly hip bump. "I want to see your place and your workshop."

"Sure, okay." I led her across the driveway and up the stairs to my apartment.

I opened the door and Ivy stepped in behind me. "This is great!" she said appreciatively, and went straight to the kitchen. "I love the soft blue cabinets, and the pops of yellow with the vintage pieces."

"The cabinets were originally white, but I wanted some color," I explained, as Sam popped out from the bedroom and, tail held high, went straight to Ivy.

"What a cool cat." Ivy held out her arms and my sturdy old cat jumped right into them. "What breed is he?"

"He's a torby." I said. "A mixture of tortoiseshell and tabby."

"I never saw a torby before." Ivy tucked a purring Sam over her shoulder and continued to walk around the apartment.

I'd never seen Sam make friends with someone so quickly. "He likes you."

"It's mutual." Ivy grinned, and checked out Eli's room. "Pirates," she said. "That figures."

"It's his obsession."

"I noticed," she said. "Think I have any chance of getting a picture of Eli without his pirate hat on?"

"Maybe, if you knock him unconscious first."

Ivy's eyes danced. "Ah, a challenge!" She poked her head into my room. "Nice," she commented, but didn't cross the threshold.

"Thank you." I sat on the end of the couch.

"Did you refinish the yellow dresser and nightstand yourself?"

"I did. They were great pieces, but they needed some love."

"The blue and yellow suits you," Ivy said. "It's homey and charming but I'm a little surprised that even in your personal space—there's not a hint of the Craft your family practices."

I smiled politely and gestured for her to join me on the sofa. "I'm sure Nathan explained to you that in our family—we are very discreet with our practices."

Ivy strolled over with the cat still in her arms. She

made herself at home, propping her feet up on the big trunk I used for a coffee table. "The rutabaga rule?" she raised an eyebrow at me. "Yeah, he did."

"Did you happen to see the Salem Village Historic District sign in downtown Danvers?" I asked, trying for patience.

"Sure," Ivy said as the cat climbed out of her lap. "We saw it. I asked Nathan to take me."

"Did you *read* the big blue sign?" I asked bluntly. "Did you see the second name listed there?"

Ivy folded her arms across her chest. "Sarah Osburn."

"That's a direct ancestor of my mother's. She was one of the first they accused, and she died in prison during the Witch trials."

"Yeah, and my ancestor Bridget Bishop was the first woman they strung up in Salem Town," Ivy said. "Not sure what is a worse way to go...being hung, or dying in a prison cell."

I huffed out a breath. "It's hardly a competition of whose family suffered more."

"Nope, it's not," Ivy said calmly. "I'm sorry if I offended you, though."

"You didn't," I said. "I'm trying to make you understand what it's like here, in Danvers."

Ivy rolled her eyes. "Trust me, your brother has been blathering on about the topic of 'discretion' ever since I met him."

"Both of our families have ties to the earliest of

Witchcraft families in America—"

"And it's interesting to me," Ivy interrupted, "how the families that moved west have ended up being more open than the ones who stayed in New England."

"Point taken."

Ivy rose to her feet and walked over to the kitchen window with the cat trailing behind her. "Your family spells their last name differently now. Was that a way to distance themselves from the trials?"

"Possibly," I admitted. "This is New England, Ivy. Danvers is an old town and my family has kept their heads down in regards to our spiritual practices and our magick for hundreds of years."

"So your legacy really is hidden." Ivy seemed to think that over.

"Yes it is. We would never reveal ourselves to a mundane. It's forbidden in my family to even discuss magick with a non-believer."

Ivy raised an eyebrow. "That's sort of a reverse type of discrimination, don't you think?"

"It's caution." I corrected her. "I agree that today more people are open to the idea of magick, but very few can accept the truth of it." I walked over to join her at the window, and we stood and watched my family below us on the lawn and back patio. "Not everyone is as fortunate as you to have the freedom to be out in the open with their practices."

"I think sometimes it's simply because there are a lot of families in William's Ford who do practice openly.

Strength in numbers, you know?" She grinned. "That and I've never been subtle. Not in my whole life, and it's not always been an easy road to walk. But it's who I am."

"I noticed." I nodded towards the big silver pentagram. "You could signal passing planes with that thing."

"My mother gave the pendant to me when I turned thirteen. I wear it to remember her and to honor what she taught me."

I shut my eyes, horrified that my attempt at humor had fallen so flat. "I'm sorry, Ivy."

"Hey," Ivy poked me in the side. "It's okay. I know you were teasing. Lighten up, Hannah."

"Can I ask you something?" I said, trying to make amends. "...from one practitioner to another?"

"Sure."

"Nathan told me you can move objects, that you're telekinetic." I waited a beat. "Is that true?"

Ivy cocked an eyebrow at me. "Damn straight, Skippy."

I smiled. "Show me."

Ivy twisted away from the window and considered the apartment. "Anything in here particularly valuable?" she asked, straight-faced.

"What?" I squeaked.

"Got ya." Ivy threw back her head and laughed.

"I suppose I walked right into—" and my words faded away. The empty plastic cup Eli had left on the counter began to rise up. It hovered about a foot above the sink.

Ivy crooked her finger and it shot straight towards her. She caught it neatly and handed it over. "Here you go."

"Wow," I managed.

"I showed you mine…" Ivy said. "So what can you do? What's *your* specialty?"

I carefully set the cup down on my kitchen table. "I'm an Air Witch."

"Meaning?"

"Meaning I have an affinity to the element of air. The wind tells me things. I have clairolfaction abilities too."

"That's the ability of psychic smell, right?" Ivy asked. "Some folks call that power clairscent?"

"Exactly," I said. "I receive psychic information by means of certain scents and smells…" I trailed off trying to figure out the best way to explain, what I'd rarely spoken aloud. "Certain fragrances mean very specific things to me. For example, when you hugged me earlier I smelled cherries and chocolate, and to me that signifies that you are truly in love with my brother."

"Jeepers." Ivy shook her head. "I'll never think of chocolate covered cherries in the same way again."

I grinned at her. "I can also manipulate the element of air to some extent."

"Oooh, show me." Ivy's eyes were bright.

I held out my hands, palms up and concentrated.

"Element of air, I call you forth," I said and the temperature in the apartment shifted dramatically.

Ivy shuddered next to me as a little breeze washed over us. It began gently, fluttering the hair back from our faces, and then a rush of wind spun clockwise around both of us. The little whirlwind picked up speed, causing my dress to snap in the wind, while Ivy tried to hold her hair out of her eyes. After a three count I allowed the elemental magick to fade out and eventually disappear all together.

Ivy whistled appreciatively. "That was bad-ass."

I drew in a deep breath and grounded, brushing my hands off from any residual energy.

The door on my apartment opened and my brother stood in the doorway frowning at us both.

CHAPTER FOUR

"What are you two doing up here?" he asked.

"Nothing," we said together, in the same tone of voice guilty children use to answer their parents.

"Careful," Nathan said, raising his eyebrows. "People will think that you're...up to something."

Ivy laughed. "Nice Professor Snape reference!"

"Relax, Nathan." I grinned at my brother. "I haven't broken any rules."

"We're just getting to know each other," Ivy said, brushing at her shirt. "You know, a little witchy show and tell."

Nathan's eyes narrowed at her, then he studied me. "You're up here doing elemental magick, Hannah?"

Ivy slung an arm around my waist. "We're only talking shop."

"Exactly," I agreed. "Shop talk."

"I'll leave you both to it." Nathan reached for the door and started to step out. "Behave yourself with the magick, Ivy," he said, mock seriously.

"Not gonna happen," Ivy snarked. "Wanna spank me later?"

"Promises, promises," Nathan said.

Caught off guard at the by-play between them, I barked out a laugh. I'd never seen my brother so relaxed and *full of fun*, I suppose was the correct term.

Ivy blew my brother a kiss and he grinned at her, closing the door behind him.

"You're good for him," I said. I could see why Nathan had fallen for Ivy Bishop—the sass and the humor were endearing.

Ivy smiled. "Thanks. It means a lot to me that you think so." She stepped back from me and surveyed the apartment as if seeing it for the first time. "Okay, *now* I get it."

"What?"

"The soft blue, yellow and white. You've surrounded yourself with the colors and symbols of the element of air." Ivy shook her head. "I'm surprised I didn't pick up on it. Usually my intuition is pretty accurate, but today, I totally missed the clues."

"There's an art to hiding your Craft in plain sight."

"It's a sort of glamour, isn't it?" Ivy decided.

"And now that you know what to look for, what do you see?" I asked, curious as to her answer.

Ivy walked around the apartment considering everything. "Well the colors for starters, and you've got a vintage, scientific chart butterfly poster above your dresser, and drawer pulls with songbirds on them in the kitchen. There's a dragonfly motif in the bathroom, all creatures associated with the element of air."

"Most people never even catch it."

"It's clever *and* sneaky. You've got to admire that." Ivy grinned. "So now I'm curious. With the clairolfaction, what sort of information do you associate with specific fragrances?"

I gestured to the kitchen table and we sat across from each other. "Well for me, love has a pretty specific scent."

"Cherries and chocolate," Ivy remembered.

"Yes, and if it's an older, more mature love...roses. Happiness smells like bubblegum, and someone who has an open, friendly way about them hits like nutmeg to me. But jealousy smells like burnt sugar, suspicion smells like mothballs, and lies or dishonesty...that comes across almost like the odor of sauerkraut." Ivy was hanging on my every word, and I had to admit it was fun to talk about my odd psychic talent with another Witch, and with a magickal practitioner who didn't think it was, well...*weird*.

"If you meet another practitioner, what does your clairolfaction tell you?"

"Well, if they're more scholarly like Nathan then I smell books and paper," I said. "If they are herbalists I detect rosemary and sage. Kitchen Witches always remind me of pumpkin spice."

Ivy chuckled at the last bit. "So if you met a Witch that specialized in candle magick, you'd probably smell smoke and melting wax?"

"Yes." I nodded. "You know, you're one of the few modern practitioners I've ever spoken to who actually understands this."

"It's cool and it's interesting." Ivy leaned forward. "So, what's danger smell like to you?"

"Ozone," I said simply.

"Shit!" Ivy's eyes went big in her face. "Can you call a storm?"

I smiled. "Not unless I lose my temper."

"Nathan told me that your grandmother, Janet Osborne, could call a storm."

"She could. The afternoon she died, a big one crashed over our town. Took out power for a few days."

"I wish I could have met her," Ivy said, and reached across the table for my hand.

"I think she would have gotten a kick out of you." I gave her fingers a squeeze. *Ivy Bishop was absolutely charming,* I decided.

"Hey, Hannah." Ivy pointed over my shoulder. "The big vintage style honey bee sign, did you make that?"

"I did."

"I really wanna see your workshop," Ivy said. "Nathan told me you have a whole online business on the side, making painted and stenciled signs."

"Sure," I said. "Let's go right down." I led the way down the stairs, and Ivy followed me into the garage—turned workshop. As I expected, she went straight for the Halloween signs that I'd started to stock up on in preparation for the October holiday.

Ivy held up a large black and white sign with distressed edges. "Not every Witch lives in Salem," she laughed at the Innkeeper style sign. "This is fabulous!"

"I figured you would go for that one," I chuckled.

"You can take a debit card, right?"

"Of course."

Ivy tucked it under her arm and rooted through the rest of the signs. She chose three others. "These are going to be gifts for my family. Good thing I brought an extra suitcase."

***

The next day was the fourth of July and it dawned hot, clear and sunny. Eli and I attended the local parade with his cousin Margot, and later that afternoon we headed over to Kayleigh and Curtis' large house for our annual family gathering. Eli was sulking, as I'd not allowed him his pirate hat, but he was outrageously pleased with the matching tie-dye patriotic shirts my mother and I had made for the whole clan.

After sundown, the family gathered together at the marina to watch the town's fireworks display out over the water. The temperatures had cooled only slightly, and fortunately the air was rarely still around the water.

Eli and I sat on a big blanket in the grass with Nathan and Ivy beside us. The rest of the family was scattered around, and Nathan was trying to convince my mother that he wasn't upset that he didn't have a matching t-shirt.

"If I would have known you were coming I'd have made you both one," she insisted as she held baby Maddie.

Ivy stretched out on the blanket in an American flag tank-top, red sandals and white shorts. "Bet you would have been *adorable* in a tie-dye shirt, Pogue."

My mother laughed and winked. "He would have been."

Eli took Ivy's prone posture as an invitation and before I could warn her, my son gave a shout and tried to dive on Ivy.

Ivy snagged him in mid-air. After a bit of a playful tussle she strolled off with him and Margot. The three of them went hand in hand towards a vendor who was selling glow in the dark bracelets.

"Have room for a couple more?"

I glanced up and saw Edmund smiling down at me. Henry Walker stood next to him, and he seemed about as pleased to see me as I felt seeing him again. "Sure," I managed.

Henry silently dropped down on the grass a few feet away. He wore cut off denim shorts and a faded navy blue t-shirt that had seen better days. He rested his elbows on his knees and lifted his face to the slight breeze coming from the port. I watched him scan the families who had gathered and felt a little prickle at the base of my neck. *He was scanning the crowd and assessing any possible problems.*

Edmund greeted Nathan and snapped out a blanket. He sat neatly between the two of us. "Hello gorgeous," he said.

"Hey handsome," I responded automatically. And he certainly was. With his red polo shirt and dark shorts, he was like an advertisement for upscale casual men's wear.

Eli came back with Ivy and Margot, and my boy happily climbed into Edmunds lap. "Edmund!" Eli cheered, snuggled right in and proceeded to bombard Edmund with the adventures of the day.

Henry watched the two of them intently. I stiffened and narrowed my eyes at Mr. Walker. The unmistakable scent of camphor—mothballs, rolled over me. This was actually psychic olfactory information, and that fragrance meant *suspicion* to me. Henry was wondering about Edmund's relationship with me—and my son.

He's trying to figure out if Edmund was Eli's father, my intuition told me. Almost as if he'd realized I knew what he was thinking, Henry shifted slightly, his attention now directly on me.

My response was a level stare. I didn't blink, I made eye contact and held it.

The corner of his mouth kicked up as if he was amused. But he returned my glare with a cool assessment of his own.

Standoff.

With another practitioner, that sort of maneuver

would have been an incredibly blatant sort of magickal power play. But Mr. Walker was no Witch. What he was, was a rude, narrow-minded son of a bitch who'd incorrectly assumed that Eli might be Edmund's son. I'd experienced this reaction before over the years...but it didn't mean that I had to like it.

Even before Edmund had come out in his college years, there had never been anything romantic between us. Edmund was like a second brother to me. We were *family*, it was that simple.

The fireworks began, and I tipped my face up to the sky, ignored the insufferable asshole to my right, and enjoyed the show. Before the display was finished, Henry Walker said something quietly to Edmund and left, disappearing into the crowd.

"Not the sociable type, is he?" I said to Edmund.

Edmund patted my hand. "Give him a chance Hannah."

I leaned into Edmunds ear as not to be overheard. "Before the fireworks started, he was wondering if you were Eli's father."

Edmund's eyebrows went way up. "What? Are you sure?"

"Trust me," I said.

"You picked that up using your intuition?" Edmund asked.

I nodded. "Absolutely." I tapped a finger along side my nose. "And he *smells* suspicious."

"Suspicious? Of what exactly?" Edmund seemed

intrigued.

"Of you and me, and our friendship."

Edmund shook his head. "I'll talk to him."

***

Since I had the following day off, I decided to take advantage of it and get some work done in my shop. Ivy and Nathan had taken Eli along with them to Salem. I knew Eli would enjoy his time with his uncle, and I'd miss my brother like crazy when he left in a couple of days. But for now I had a lot of signs to make and, happily, most of the day to myself.

I tossed on my oldest white tank top and gray gym shorts. They were a tad too small from being washed and dried too many times—but they were comfortable. Since no one would see me, I ditched my makeup and pulled my hair back in a long ponytail. I lifted the garage door open, switched on a box fan to keep the July air circulating, and began to prep boards. I put my protective glasses on, tucked my ear buds in place, cranked up some rock, and got to work. I measured out the pine boards, set up my portable work table and took out my circular saw. I clamped the boards in place and began cutting the signs to the desired lengths.

I turned off the saw, picked up the short stack of boards from the garage floor and carried them over to my belt sander. I stacked them neatly, flipped the switch and began sanding the edges of the wooden signs smooth. The garage smelled of pine dust and summer. Sweat dripped down my back and I ignored it. I was singing along to my music and finishing a large board when a little puff of air hit me in the nape of the neck: The element's way of warning me that I was no longer alone. A new scent caught my attention: Brine, sand, and the smell of the ocean.

I glanced over my shoulder and found Henry Walker standing hipshot in the open garage door with his thumbs tucked in his front pockets. He looked rumpled and scruffy in disreputable jeans and a faded red shirt. His hair tumbled into his eyes, and he wore mirrored sunglasses and attitude.

Intuitively I knew his gun was secured at the small of his back. Why in the world he thought he'd need to be carrying a gun in the 'burbs of Danvers, I had no idea.

Annoyed, I tugged out an earbud. *What are you doing here?* I wanted to ask. Instead, I bit that off and said, "Yes?"

"Edmund told me where to find you." He pitched his voice to be heard over the noise.

"I'm working," I said over the belt sander. For spite, I turned my back on him.

He moved along side of me at the workbench. "I'd like to talk to you," he said, stretching his arm across to flip the power switch on the belt sander.

I smacked his hand away before he could accidentally hurt himself. "Hands away from the equipment!" I snapped.

He held his hands up, and took a step back.

"Give me a minute," I said over the noise, and proceeded to finish the edges of the board. I held the edge of the board to the sander and pressed down. After a five count I lifted it and ran a testing finger across the wood. I nodded, satisfied with the smooth edge. I shut down the sander, stacked the board on top of the others. I switched my music off and finally swiveled to face him. "Talk," I said.

"I only want to say this once," he began, and quicker than I could react, he looped his finger through the wire to my remaining earbud and tugged it out.

I batted his hand away. "Hands off."

His mouth kicked up. "Wanted to make sure you could hear me."

I shoved the safety glasses on top my head. "You are, without a doubt, the rudest man I have *ever* met."

"Listen darlin'—"

"In my *entire* life," I spoke right over him.

His brows lowered. "You gonna let me apologize, or keep interrupting?"

I crossed my arms over my chest and waited.

"Edmund spoke to me last night." He took his sunglasses off and set them on an open space on my workbench. "He told me about your boy's father."

I tipped my head over to the side, but said nothing.

"I'm sorry for your loss," he said. "I also wanted to apologize. I jumped to the wrong conclusions about your relationship with Edmund. He explained that you've been friends since you were kids."

You're not the first—" I stopped myself from saying *idiot*, and changed the word at the last second, "person to assume that. Some people simply can't wrap their mind around a man and woman being friends...but let me make something clear, Mr. Walker. Edmund and I are more than friends. We're *family*."

He nodded. "Understood."

I silently counted to ten, as he continued to just *stand there*. Finally, I'd had enough. "Well this has been lovely, but I have to get back to work." I gestured towards the open garage door. "There's the door Mr. Walker. I'm sure you can find your way out." I pulled the safety glasses back down and turned my back in dismissal.

Instead of leaving, he stepped closer and considered the stacks of recently sanded boards on the workbench. "What are you doing in here, anyway?"

"Baking cupcakes," I snarked, picking up the circular saw from the bench.

"You're going to hurt yourself with that," he said.

I was sorely tempted to pull the trigger on the saw for a second, so it would come on with a loud grind. But considering that he was armed, that might not be my smartest move. Instead, I unplugged the saw and wound up the cord. "Trust me, I know how to handle power tools." I said through my teeth.

"Did you cut all these boards up yourself?" He

seemed genuinely surprised.

I rolled my eyes at the chauvinist question. "Of course."

He scanned the sander, and drill press, and finally seemed to put all the pieces together. "*You're* actually doing woodworking?"

I flared my eyes wide at him. "Wow, with that level of deductive ability, the local criminals should be shaking in their shoes! I mean honestly, what was your first clue? The boards, the sander I was using, or the sawdust I'm currently covered in?"

"Guess you told me." He snorted out a laugh and he smiled. A real smile, and when he did...it changed everything about him.

It must have been some sort of magick, but the smile made the casual clothes seem charmingly scruffy—as opposed to messy. The smile added some appeal to those roguish green eyes, and I felt a little twitch in my belly in reaction.

And that annoyed the hell out of me.

"Okay, so you apologized," I said, ungraciously. "Now go. I have work to do."

"Maybe I'm curious, it's not every day you meet a woman who can handle power tools."

"Do you mean to be sexist or can you simply not help yourself?" I sputtered.

"Most women I know appreciate a compliment."

"I imagine the ones *you* know, do. However, I've yet to hear one from you."

"Are you fishing for a compliment, darlin'?"

"Is this your version of Southern charm?" I asked.

"Is it working?" he asked cheerfully.

"No," I told him. "It most definitely is not." That slow drawl was getting on my last good nerve, and yet, I struggled not to smile.

Unfazed, he started poking around the garage. "So is this woodworking a hobby or something? What are you making?"

"I'm making signs. Decorative signs," I explained. "I sell them at my parent's shop and online."

"You got any finished ones in here?"

"Yes, I do," I said, pointing to the area where I stored the finished signs.

With that he walked over to the opposite side of the garage where the boxes of signs were stacked together and waiting to be shipped out. He made himself at home and starting rooting through them.

"I like this one." He held up a pirate themed sign.

"I can't tell you how much your approval means to me." I tucked my ear buds back in and hit play. I plugged in the shop-vac and turned it on, cleaning up the saw dust from my work table and bench. I took my time, even though it was miserably hot in the garage, and I fully expected him to be gone by the time I finished cleaning up.

It was probably not my best move, being so rude to the man...Considering that I had to work with him. Sure he had tried to apologize, but he'd barged into my workshop, asking all sorts of stupid questions...Then he had to go all Southern charm, and smile at me, and the fact that I'd reacted to it...that really pissed me off more than anything else.

My mind went back and forth, and by the time I finished with the shop-vac, I was relieved to find that he'd left.

Cleanup finished, I clicked off the fan and headed out on the back patio. Everyone was out for the day, and I eyeballed the garden hose. I was miserably hot, itchy, and the idea of trailing all that sawdust into the apartment didn't appeal to me. I kicked off my shoes, took off my iPod, rolled up the cords to the earbuds and tucked them inside one of my shoes.

Barefoot, I jogged over to the faucet, turned on the water, and carried the hose across the grass. I waited a few moments for the cold water to run through the hose. I tested the temperature of the water, found it cool, and took a couple of swigs. W*hat the hell,* I decided, and held the hose right over my head.

The shock of the cold water had me gasping, but it felt fantastic. I tipped my head back, closed my eyes as the water rushed over my face. Next, I aimed the hose down my neck and back, shuddering in relief. Keeping my eyes closed, I tugged my shirt away from my cleavage and let the water run right down my front. The icy water washed away all the sawdust that had clung to my bra and chest. It was a childish pleasure, but fun, nonetheless.

In a much better mood, I swiped the water away from eyes, wrung out my ponytail, and decided to water my mother's butterfly gardens while I was at it. A few Painted Lady butterflies fluttered around as I held the hose at the base of some purple coneflowers. A flirty yellow Swallowtail danced around me and settled on my shoulder.

"Hello, there," I said to the butterfly. As if my words were an invitation, several more landed on me.

I moved slowly in deference to my passengers, taking my time and watering all the plants. After a little while, I was only slightly dripping, so I finished up with the garden and went to go turn the water off. I twisted the faucet, turned and managed about three steps and froze, when I realized I wasn't alone after all.

Henry Walker stood in the shade of the back patio, silently watching me. About a million thoughts raced through my head. *Why was he still here? Why was he watching me...Oh crap, the thin white tank I'd worn was practically transparent...thank goddess I had a bra on...*And finally...*I hoped he hadn't thought that my cooling off with the hose, was some sort of teasing exhibition.*

"I thought I was alone," I said, and the butterflies took off in a colorful, fluttering swirl between the two of us.

We stood staring at each other for a heartbeat, then two.

"You had butterflies all over you," he said very

quietly.

I hooked a thumb over my shoulder towards the flowers I'd watered. "Well, that *is* a butterfly garden." I tried hard to make my voice sound casual.

"Never saw anything like that before." His eyes were steady, but the cautious tone put me on guard.

"Why are you still here?"

"I left my sunglasses. Came back to get them." He held them up. "I was surprised when you came out here to cool off."

"As I said, I thought I was *alone*."

"Gotta say, you're the last person I would have expected to have hosed off in the back yard."

I refused to be embarrassed, but I still wanted him to go away. "Well, if you'll excuse me, I need to get cleaned up before my son comes home."

He stepped back and slipped his shades back on. "Sure, I'll see you at the office."

I nodded to him, and he left. I stayed where I was, waiting until I heard his car drive away. I blew out a breath as a Viceroy butterfly landed on my nose.

"That was a close one," I said to the Viceroy, who flapped its wings in answer and flew away. Relieved that he'd taken my winged friends as simply a by-product of a butterfly garden, I picked up my shoes and iPod, and headed up the back steps.

I made the top landing and the wind chimes by the door began to clang and ring. The sound they made was slightly mocking, and I knew the element of air was laughing at my predicament.

CHAPTER FIVE

When I arrived at the agency on Monday morning, it was precisely nine o'clock. I'd given myself a pep talk on the way to work, and I was determined to be as polite and professional as possible.

In an effort to present myself as a lady, I wore a patterned swing dress in navy and coral. In deference to the July heat, it hit at the knees and was sleeveless. To jazz it up a bit, I'd worn my grandmother's enameled butterfly locket and some coral colored sandals.

I heard throbbing music as I unlocked the front door, but assumed it was from a passing car. When I opened the door however, the volume of the music punched out and I took a step back. "What the hell?" I muttered. The racket was coming from *inside* our agency, and it only took a second to identify the culprit.

Henry Walker appeared to be reorganizing his new office. The room had originally been used for storage, and Edmund had a desk and filing cabinets brought in for his friend last week. But at the moment there was—

goddess preserve us—country music blaring loud enough to almost drown out the phone that was ringing on my desk.

While the singer on the radio wailed about cruising through little farm towns with his windows down, I shut the door behind me and rushed to grab the phone. "Fox Investigations, hold please," I said over the music, and punched the hold button without waiting for a reply. I dumped my purse on my desk and marched over to his office.

A beat up old boom box balancing on top a maple filing cabinet was the source of the obnoxious music. Instead of wasting time trying to turn it down, I grabbed the cord and yanked the plug straight out of the wall.

The silence was instant and exquisite.

"Good morning." Henry grinned at me and, to my amazement, kept singing as if the music was still playing.

His voice wasn't bad, but the grin really pissed me off. "It's business hours, Mr. Walker. The music—if that's what you can call it—needs to be turned off." I heard my own words and winced internally. *I sounded like some prissy librarian.* That realization only aggravated me more.

"Darlin', you don't like country music?"

"Don't call me *darlin'*." I dropped the plug and it bounced off the hardwood floor. "Business hours are from 9:00 am until 4:30 pm," I told him.

"I'll keep that in mind," he drawled.

I caught myself grinding my teeth and with an effort, unclenched my jaw. "Thank you." I spun on my heel and went to see if the caller on hold had waited.

Thus began two weeks of hell at the agency.

The man seemed determined to annoy the crap out of me in whatever way he could. After a few days, calls started coming in for Henry as well as Edmund. If Henry was in the office, I transferred the calls and buzzed them through to him.

If he was out, I took the messages and left them on his desk with a neon colored sticky note, as I did for Edmund.

Henry strolled past me one afternoon and told me—in his Southern twang—that he hated bright colors. Then he crumpled up the notes, dropped them in my wastebasket, and strolled off.

Undeterred, I began texting him his phone messages when he was out of the office.

I don't know why I bothered, he rarely returned those messages either...which meant I was faced with an ever growing list of very annoyed people on the phone. In retaliation I taped a huge hot pink note on his desk informing him that if he did not start returning his calls or acknowledging that he had received a text from me about a client—that I would start giving out his private cell phone number—so the callers could reach him directly twenty-four hours a day.

Edmund laughed off the neon note thing, shrugged over Henry's lack of organization, and I tried not to let it get to me. I suspected it was all an enormous ploy by Henry Walker to annoy the hell out of me, and damn it, it was really working.

My sister called me in a panic at the end of the second week of insanity and asked if I could watch the baby for a few hours. I knew Edmund wouldn't mind, and Henry was out doing whatever it was that he did, so I told her to drop by the agency.

Kayleigh blew into the office. She had her two month old with her, a diaper bag, and a portable crib.

"Sorry!" she plopped the diaper bag on my desk. "The babysitter has a bug, and Curtis is showing houses this morning." She balanced the baby in one arm and set the port-a-crib on the floor with the dexterity only a mother of small children can manage. My sister was tall and stunning. You'd never have guessed she'd had a baby a few months ago. Her brown hair was pulled back in a sleek ponytail, but her gray eyes were tired.

"Rough night?" I asked.

"Just when I thought I had her sleeping through the night." She blew her bangs out of her eyes and held the baby out. "Are you sure you don't mind?"

"Gimme," I said, reaching for my niece. I tossed a burp pad over the shoulder of my black summer dress and held the baby, while my older sister bustled around and got the baby stuff all set up. While Kayleigh tucked a bottle in the mini fridge and told me the last time the baby had eaten, my niece stared solemnly up at me. "Hi Maddie," I said and kissed her cheek. One side of the baby's mouth lifted up, which made me grin.

"Curtis should be finished by noon," Kayleigh said. "So he'll swing by and pick up the baby, and go get Margot and Eli from daycare this afternoon."

"Sounds good," I said.

Kayleigh lifted her head and sniffed the air. "Damn, that coffee smells wonderful. I'd *kill* for a coffee."

"There's the machine in the back, help yourself." I glanced up from the baby and smiled as Kayleigh groaned dramatically. "You can have a decaf while you're nursing," I pointed out.

"Don't have the time. I'm late for my dentist appointment...have to get that stupid cavity fixed. Thanks again Hannah, I owe you." With that, she blew me a kiss and bolted out the door.

Maddie seemed content to be held, so I sat at the desk with my niece tucked in my arm and worked my way through the case files Edmund had asked me to review. There had been a few more burglaries in the affluent Oak Hills neighborhood. One, I realized as my stomach sank, only a few doors down from where my sister lived with her family.

I felt a little tingle at the base of my neck and my clairolfaction kicked in as I read through the files. I picked up on the scent of stale beer, and smoke. Not cigarette smoke—smoke from a fire. Concerned, I read through the case files carefully and noticed that the local police still didn't have any specific leads, though they believed it was a group of people working together.

The scent of smoke stayed with me, so I swiveled the chair towards my computer and typed in a search one-handed, checking to see if there was any mention of fires, or even if there were any active arson investigations in the area.

"Hmmm," I murmured as Maddie waved her hands and kicked her feet, "I think this may be more than a few teens looking for a thrill."

Maddie responded with a gurgling coo and a gigantic yawn.

"I know, right?" I said to her, and jolted when a shadow fell across my desk. Henry Walker stood blocking the light from the front window, and frowning down at me.

"We take on a new client while I was out?" he drawled.

"In a way," I said calmly. "I'm emergency babysitting for my sister. Her husband will be here to pick up the baby in an hour."

Henry grunted at that. He stepped away from my desk and spotted the open case files. "Are those the files from the Oak Hills Homeowners Association?"

"They are."

"Why do *you* have them?"

I made sure that when I spoke my voice would be pleasant. "Edmund asked me to look them over." I waited to see if he would make a rude comment about me reading them.

Henry rolled his eyes. "Still playing consultant, are we?"

At least the man was predictable. I thought and reminded myself to be polite. "I assure you, Mr. Walker," I said, "I am *not* playing."

Henry's eyes narrowed as he considered me sitting at my desk with the baby. "I still can't get a read on you Hannah," he said.

I glanced up at him, as if shocked. "You can read?"

"You go right ahead with that smart mouth, I'll figure out what it is that you're hiding."

It took everything I had not to react to his words.

Edmund strolled in the front door. "Hey, Maddie's here!" He grinned from ear to ear. "Give me that baby," he said, scooping her right out of my arms.

"You running a daycare center on the side, bro?" Henry rolled his eyes at Edmund.

Edmund made an anatomically impossible suggestion to Henry, in the politest tone I'd ever heard, and I gawked as Henry began to laugh.

"You shouldn't talk like that in front of a baby," Henry said—taking the words right out of my mouth.

Edmund smiled, but instead of responding to Henry he spoke to me. "Hannah did you get a chance to go over the Oak Hills case?"

"I did." I gathered up the files and stacked them neatly.

"Impressions?" Edmund asked.

I slanted my eyes from Henry's suspicious face to

Edmund's back as he gently lay the now snoozing baby in her port-a-crib. "Ah, I do have a few."

Henry shrugged and went into his office, but left the door open.

Edmund picked up a chair and set it by the corner of my desk. His eyes fell on my computer screen, and what I'd been searching. "Tell me."

"I don't think this is bored teens looking for something to do," I said, checking to make sure Henry was still in his office. "I picked up on the scent of stale beer and smoke."

"Like from cigarettes?" Edmund asked.

"Not cigarette smoke," I said, anticipating him, "I mean *smoke*, smoke. As in from a fire."

"Your intuition's telling you, the thieves are about to up their game?"

"Yes," I said, keeping my voice low. "I think they may try arson next."

"Shit." Edmund blew out a breath.

"This is Kayleigh and Curtis' neighborhood. The last burglary was three houses down from them," I reminded him.

"They've got a security system, right?"

I nodded. "Curtis put one in when the first robberies happened in June."

"Maybe you should talk to Curtis when he picks up Maddie," Edmund suggested. "Tell him to be vigilant, and to keep his eyes open."

"I will," I said. "I really hope I'm wrong about the

smoke..." I trailed off, glancing over at my niece who snoozed on her back.

Edmund squinted at the computer. "I've never known you to be wrong before when you put your *nose* to work on a case."

"Bloodhounds are us," I joked.

"I still think we should have named the agency, *Fox and Hound Investigations*," Edmund said completely seriously.

"No. Not with my dog allergies." I laughed at the long standing joke and went back to work.

An hour later and my brother-in-law had picked up Maddie. As he loaded up the baby in her car seat I passed along Edmund's advice to keep his eyes open. I stood on the sidewalk in front of the agency and waved as he drove off. Scanning the street, I was delighted by the brisk foot traffic.

As a matter of fact, there was a nice crowd in my parent's shop across the road. While I stood there, I noticed a group of teenagers hanging out on the corner. The three boys laughed too loudly, and took turns insulting each other.

I reached blindly for the front door only to bounce off the chest of Henry Walker.

"Excuse me," I said automatically.

Henry reached out to steady me, wrapping his hand around my elbow. "What were you staring at?" he asked.

I pointed towards the spice shop. "The kids on the

corner, and my parent's shop. They're busy today."

"I'm headed out on a case," he said and dropped his hand.

"Do you have your cell phone?" I asked automatically.

"Yes ma'am," he smirked at me. "You sound like my..."

The breeze shifted and I caught the bitter odor of sauerkraut. *Dishonesty.* I narrowed my eyes, tuned out Henry's voice, and considered the boys a bit more carefully. The trio had begun walking towards my parent's shop.

I couldn't say what had my attention so riveted on the group of teenagers. But when the scent of ozone hit me, I stopped questioning my reaction. My intuition was screaming at me that something was very wrong...and I had never experienced catching the scent of ozone without a damn good reason.

"...are you even listening to me?" Henry asked.

"No, I'm not." I waved him away. *My mother was working alone today,* I recalled staring at their store front. My heart began to speed up. *She was in danger.* "Excuse me, I'm going to go check on something."

"What are you talking about?"

I ignored him, saw that I had a break in the traffic, lifted the hem of my skirt, and jogged across the road in my practical flats.

I opened the door and stepped around the shoppers who were exiting with their purchases. They filed out, leaving the door wide open to the afternoon sunshine. The teens, I discovered, had spread out across the sales floor. One of the boys was wearing an oversized jacket, and he was loitering very near the racks of cookies and candies. Another boy, wearing a ball cap and baggy shorts, was standing next to the cash register, and the third of the boys was asking my mother all sorts of questions. *Keeping her distracted,* I knew.

A new smell hit me, and it was a metallic smell, with traces of gunpowder. *One of those boys had a gun...* I knew intuitively, and my heart leapt to my throat in reaction. To my surprise Henry Walker stepped in, right behind me. He nodded and eased over to the right side of the store.

"Hi Mom!" I said loudly. "Gosh, you sure are busy today!" Smiling broadly, I headed for the counter, snagging the shop's oversized broom on my way. Despite the fact that the broom was decorated with a big spray of dried herbs, its handle was heavy, thick and made of oak. "Can I help you?" I said, making eye contact with the kid loitering by the register.

The teen recoiled, and started swinging his eyes around, checking to see where his friends were. "Uh, no. No, I'm good," he stammered. "It's cool."

"You sure?" I asked, never taking my eyes off him, even as I felt a little breeze begin to ruffle my hair. Uncalled, the element of air wrapped itself around me —which sometimes happened whenever I was really angry, or afraid as I was now. The little airstream picked up in intensity, rolled towards the boy, and his eyes went huge. I watched as his mind tried to work out what was happening.

He glanced from the broom and back to my eyes, and he paled. "Witch," he whispered.

Saying nothing, I smiled at him very slowly, and he stumbled back.

"Let's go guys," he called to his friends.

The kid who'd been peppering my mother with questions stopped and considered his buddies.

The third boy in the big jacket nodded and moved towards the door. I watched Henry shift his body, and the minute the kid stepped over the threshold, he grabbed him by the collar and yanked him back inside.

The kid in the jacket took a swing at Henry, who dodged it easily. "You don't want to do that son," he said. Henry bent the kid's arm behind him, applying pressure.

"Mom, call the police!" I pushed out with one hand, the door slammed shut, and I swung out from behind the counter.

"Ow!" the kid yelled at Henry. "What are you? A cop or something?"

Henry applied a bit more pressure, and the kid stopped struggling. His knees hit the ground, and packages of candy and boxed cookies fell out from under his jacket to the floor of the shop.

I could hear my mother in the background, her voice was high pitched and she was speaking very quickly into the phone. I checked the other two boys. The pale boy who'd stood by the register held his hands up in the air and backed away from me. "It was *his* idea!" He pointed to the third boy. "I didn't do anything!" he insisted, "I didn't do *anything*!"

"Shut up, Zane," growled the third boy. He made no move to run, but there was something in his stance that had my mouth drying up.

I focused on him. The third teen was only a few feet away from me, and I picked up the scent of metal and gunpowder *again*. I glanced at my mother. She was standing way too close to him, and was still on the phone with the 911 operator. "Mom," I called to her, and she swung her eyes towards me. "Ozone," I said.

My mother's eyes flared wide, and she hit the floor.

The third boy started to reach around to his back, and several things seemed to happen at once: Henry started to shove the boy he'd collared to the floor. The second kid, Zane, started screaming, and without a plan in mind...I pushed out with the broom handle—hard—and popped the kid that was reaching for a gun, right on the end of his nose.

There was a nasty crunching sound, and he dropped to his knees, the gun clattering to the hardwood floor. Blood poured from his nose, and Henry leapt to secure the fallen gun.

"Are you crazy?" Henry snarled at me. "What were you thinking?"

My stomach lurched at the smell of the fresh blood.

"He was going for a gun," I pointed out.

"Oh my god, oh my god..." Zane repeated over and over again. He'd also dropped to his knees and put his hands behind his head. Clearly Zane knew the drill.

My mother came around the counter with a baseball bat and few heavy duty zip ties. "Here," she said, handing them calmly to Henry. "I imagine you can use these to secure that young man who had the gun."

I gaped in shock at my mother. There she stood, our family drama queen, as cool as a cucumber, while I was shaking in reaction. The boy in the jacket shifted on the floor, and I turned to him, raising the broom handle. "Don't move," I warned him with a wobbly voice.

"I'd listen to her if I were you," Henry advised as he secured the bleeding boy's wrists behind his back. "Unless you'd like her to break *your* nose while she's at it."

Zane cringed away from me. "Holy shit, she's a real *Witch*."

"Hannah," my mother said, patting me on the shoulder, "maybe you should sit down, you're awfully pale." She went to stand over the two other boys who were now on the floor, sitting on their hands.

"I'm okay," I managed, and tried not to be sick from the combination of the spices in the shop *and* the smell of the blood.

"Popped him in the nose with the broom! Wait until I tell your father!" My mother laughed. "That's my girl!"

Henry straightened and glanced over at my mother.

He shook his head and assessed me with hard green eyes. "You took a hell of a risk..." he began to lecture, but before he could continue, the sounds of the sirens from the arriving police cut him off.

***

The resulting pandemonium took hours to straighten out. The third boy had to first be taken to the local hospital to treat his broken nose, while the other two boys were taken directly to the police station.

I'd probably still be making statements and being interviewed by the police if it weren't for a few very good reasons: Number one, the store had a video surveillance system in place and the whole thing had been caught on tape. Number two, Zane and the boy who'd attempted to shoplift the cookies and candies had both started talking to save themselves from an attempted armed robbery charge...and the third reason? Henry Walker.

Once Henry's credentials were established as an ex-cop and a current private detective, the entire mood of the interviews changed. When I was finally allowed to leave, I went straight back to the agency, gathered up my things and left. It didn't hit me until I pulled up into my sister's driveway to pick up my son—all the things that could have gone wrong. Then I sat and shook in reaction for a while.

I loaded Eli in the car and thanked my lucky stars

that Kayleigh had been on the phone with my mother getting her version of the events. Otherwise I'd have never gotten out of there so easily. Curtis had waited until I finished buckling Eli in, dropped a kiss on my cheek, and announced that he was proud of me.

My cell phone was blowing up, so I switched it to silent and decided to take Eli to the Marina, and to *Mona's Lobster Shack*, for his favorite dinner. We sat at a four top table under the shade of an umbrella, and I listened while he filled me in on his adventures at daycare.

"What's wrong Mama?" Eli asked.

I started to say, *nothing*, but couldn't bring myself to lie to my little boy. Goddess knows he'd hear about the incident at the spice shop soon enough. So I decided to keep it light. "Grandma had some excitement at the shop today..." I began, and made an effort to make the whole thing sound silly instead of scary.

Eli giggled. "You really hit the bad guy in the nose with Grandma's big broom?"

"Yeah, I did," I admitted.

"Did it go *crunch*?"

I smiled. "It sure did. Nobody messes with our family and gets away with it."

"Are the bad guys in jail?" Eli's eyes were round with excitement.

"Yes," I said, keeping it simple.

"You're like Batman," Eli announced.

"No I'm not," I said. "And besides, I wasn't alone.

Mr. Walker was there and he helped your grandma and me."

"Who's Mr. Walker?" Eli asked, slurping his soda through a straw.

"I am," came Henry's voice from off to our left.

Henry Walker strolled right up and sat down in an empty chair across from me. "Hannah." He nodded.

Eli's eyes had grown large in his face. Stuck, I introduced my son. "Eli, this is Henry Walker. Remember I told you that he works with Edmund at the agency."

Eli set his soda down on the table. "Mama says you helped catch the bad guys today."

"Well your Mama helped too," Henry told Eli.

Eli dove back into his french fries. "Nobody messes with our family," Eli said, repeating my words.

Henry's lips twitched. "I'll keep that in mind."

Go away, I thought. I didn't want him there. What I wanted was to wind down from the afternoon's events, not have to deal with his misgivings and disapproval. "We're eating our supper," I said as politely as I could manage. "If you'll excuse us, Mr. Walker?"

"I was hoping to talk to you about this afternoon." Henry kicked back in his chair, clearly in no rush to leave.

"That will have to wait until tomorrow," I said firmly.

Bottle green eyes assessed me, and my stomach dropped. *He'd seen something.* I realized. I'd tried to be careful with my powers, but in the heat of the moment I'd only been concerned with keeping my mother safe.

"Fine. We can talk tomorrow at the office." He stood. "See you around kid," he said to Eli and ambled off down the marina and towards his sailboat.

"That's the pirate," Eli said, watching him walk away with very large eyes.

"He's not a pirate, Eli," I said as patiently as I could manage.

Eli shifted back to me. "Captain Time thinks he is."

"Finish your chicken fingers," I suggested.

CHAPTER SIX

I spent the morning answering dozens of phone calls. Unfortunately they weren't clients for the agency. Instead it was curious neighbors and friends of the family who'd heard about the incident at the spice shop and wanted to talk to me about it.

Between phone calls, I attempted to keep the office in order. Edmund had a court appearance this morning, otherwise I knew he would have been having a few words with me about yesterday. He'd said as much when I'd finally taken my phone off silent the night before.

To my relief, Henry Walker had not graced me with his presence as of yet. For all I knew he was on his boat, out on a case, or, I thought, sleeping upstairs in his apartment. As if my thoughts had conjured him up, I heard him coming down the stairs. I straightened my shoulders and reminded myself I'd protected my mother, defended myself from physical harm, and hadn't done anything with my magick that couldn't be explained away.

Probably.

I was pretty sure of that, anyway.

Henry went straight to the coffee machine and made himself a cup. I could see out of the corner of my eye that he had a notebook tucked under his arm, and once he had his coffee, he stopped in the doorway of the kitchenette, leaned against it and regarded me thoughtfully.

"Good morning," I said.

"Hannah." He sipped his coffee and continued to stare at me. Today he wore a gray t-shirt with a short sleeved blue plaid shirt unbuttoned over the top. His jeans were faded and torn at the knee. I appreciated all over again just how attractive the man was.

Damn it.

The stare was getting on my nerves, and I knew that *he* knew it. "You said you wanted to speak to me?" I asked, taking the bull by the horns.

"I do." He tipped his head towards his door. "Step in my office, please."

I stood and went to his office. I sat in the one chair for clients and smoothed my soft gray maxi dress over my lap.

Henry joined me and opened up the little electronic notebook. He propped it up to a standing position and began to type in a few commands. In a few moments a video flickered to life. It was the surveillance footage from my parent's store.

I lifted my eyes to his and waited for him to speak.

"I've gone over this footage dozens of times since last night," Henry said carefully. "There's a few things on it that don't add up for me."

I resisted the urge to cross my arms over my chest. That was a defensive posture, and he'd take that as confirmation that I was hiding something. "Oh?" I asked and leaned forward as if I was curious. *Don't react, don't react.* I repeated to myself.

Henry perched a hip on his desk and watched me as I studied the video. There was no sound, and the security recording wasn't crystal clear—and for that I was profoundly grateful. "In this spot here," he said tapping a key and pausing the video. "The door to the shop slams shut. All by itself."

"It does?" I did my best to sound surprised. I waited while Henry rewound the video, and I watched again, as if fascinated. "Hmm...I guess the wind caught it," I said, completely honest.

Well, that was the truth. The wind did catch it.

"Then there's this little section here," he said, rewinding the recording. He pointed to the screen and I saw myself facing off with the teenager named Zane from across the counter.

Luckily, it was barely noticeable the way my hair and long black dress had rippled. *Unless you were watching for something unusual.* It didn't show up at all on the recording how the element of air had rolled towards the boy, but you could see his facial expression, and the fear in his eyes as he'd stepped away from me.

"What am I supposed to be looking for?" I frowned up at him, as if confused.

"Maybe that confused frown works on the locals around here darlin', but it sure as hell don't work on me," Henry drawled.

The recording rolled forward and the section came up again to the part that showed the door slamming. Unfortunately, the video *had* caught me pushing my hand out a second before the door closed.

"I want to know how you did that." He angled his head towards the recording.

Deflect and distract, I braced myself. "Did what?" I asked, tucking my hair behind my ear.

He hissed out a breath in frustration. "How you scared that kid into stepping back from you. How you seemed to shut the door from across the room, and most of all I want to know how you knew that third kid had a gun—even before I did."

"What makes you think that *I* knew he was armed?"

"Responding with a question is a classic way to avoid answering the original question."

"It is?" I said as wide eyed and breathless as possible. "Goodness, it's almost like I work with a Private Investigator!"

"Cut that shit out."

I smiled, and batted my eyes at him for effect.

"You knew he was armed. You warned your mother."

His brows lowered and he leaned forward. "Was *ozone* a code word y'all had worked out in case of a robbery?"

"No, it's not a code word," I said.

Henry was rapidly losing his composure. "Did you see his gun?"

"No I didn't see it." I sighed.

"Then how did you know?"

Maybe the truth was the best cover after all. "I smelled it on him."

My answer didn't sit very well with Henry. "No more games, Hannah. Let's start again."

"Interrogation tactics really won't work on me," I said pleasantly.

Henry swore under his breath.

"Are you accusing me of something, Mr. Walker?" I asked, and was proud that I'd managed to keep my voice at an even pitch, even as his temper visibly unraveled.

Henry glared at me, and I met that glare with a neutral expression. It wasn't easy keeping my expression relaxed, but I pulled it off. Thankfully, the phone on my desk began to ring. I stood up. "Excuse me, I need to answer that."

"We aren't finished, Hannah," he said blocking the exit.

Stand off. Practically nose to nose we measured each other. He bent down, searching my eyes, and I tipped my chin up, reminding myself to breathe through my mouth. The last thing I wanted to do was get a whiff of how angry or suspicious he was of me.

He stood staring down at me for a few seconds longer, and for one wild moment I wondered if he was about to kiss me. It was in his eyes, and I yanked my head back in refusal. It seemed like forever until he finally eased away.

I took a cautions step to the left. The phone continued to ring, and Henry reluctantly shifted aside.

I went to my desk and answered the phone. It was a reporter from the local paper wanting to interview me. I was so rattled by the confrontation with Henry that I let him talk longer than I should have. Once I finally clued into what the reporter was saying, I cut the call short. "No comment," I said, and hung up. I forced myself to sit in my chair. I straightened up the files on my desk and began to generate the payroll reports.

The fact that I accomplished absolutely nothing for a half hour didn't matter. Because when Henry left all he saw was me working my way through the payroll. My stomach was tied into knots, and I breathed a sigh of relief when he walked out.

Now that he was gone, I played over the whole scene in my mind. Had he really thought he could intimidate me into confessing *something*? Did he even understand what he was poking around the edges of? My temper started to bubble and boil.

The papers on my desk began to flutter in the wind that my temper had called into the office. I slapped my hands down on them to keep them from blowing away and worked to calm down. *Holy shit! If that would've happened while he was in the office...*Horrified, I took a deep breath and tried to ground and center my energy.

The wind died down and I rolled my shoulders, trying to find some relief from the tension that had gathered there.

The truth was, I reminded myself. *He didn't know exactly what he was seeing on that video, and for that, he should consider himself damn lucky.* Because I would have defended myself, by whatever means necessary, and he wouldn't have enjoyed the experience. Not at all.

What Mr. Walker hadn't counted on was when you try and force a modern-day Witch to confess...they were going to do one of three things: Deflect attention and confuse their opponent, try and charm their way out of the situation, or if they had no other choice—hex the be-jesus out of their accuser.

The last thought made me flinch. *I sincerely hoped it wouldn't come to that.* I saw movement outside of the agency's front windows. The door was yanked open and a stunning woman walked in. Her hair was dyed a deep burgundy and it trailed down her shoulders in long waves. A black and red floral pattern sundress flowed around a trim figure. Amber colored eyes took in the room, and her deeply painted mouth smiled when she spotted me sitting at my desk.

She could best be described in one word: Bombshell.

"Hello Rowan." I smiled at my cousin.

"There you are." She went directly to me, drew me up out of my chair and pulled me in for a hug. "Heard about the big caper yesterday. I'm so glad you're safe."

Her scent was all campfires and smoked spice. Rowan Osborne was a Fire Witch, and she simply radiated energy, heat and sexuality. Rowan was a free spirit, Bohemian, and the wild child of the family. A talented makeup artist and hairstylist, she definitely walked to her own drum. She was, I supposed, our very own version of Ivy Bishop.

"I'm okay," I said, hugging her back and taking comfort.

"You're sending out some very distressed and pissed off vibes," she whispered in my ear.

"Sorry, it's been a tough twenty-four hours."

"Girl, I felt you all the way across town about an hour ago," she said, letting me out of her hug. "What was going on?"

"I had to bluff my way past the new partner here at the agency."

"The Henry Walker guy?" My cousin arched one perfect eyebrow. "What happened?"

"He was studying the security camera footage from the spice shop, and I'm on it."

Rowan's expertly painted eyes widened. "Aunt Maryanne told me that you'd called on your element during the robbery, to scare one of those kids. How much did Walker see?"

"It's not too bad, the footage isn't at a good

angle...however, he's seen enough to start questioning."

"Son of a bitch," Rowan muttered, running a hand down my arm. "Are you going to have to spell him?"

"I hope not," I said. "I'm worried though. I came very close to exposure yesterday during the robbery."

"Fuck that." Rowan gave my hand a bolstering squeeze. "You know damn good and well when it comes to self-defense the non-disclosure rule can be bent."

"I know, I just didn't expect that he would put it all together, or so quickly." I rubbed the base of my neck were my muscles had tightened into knots.

"Where's Edmund?" Rowan asked.

"He's at court testifying in a case today."

"Get your purse," Rowan ordered. "I'm taking you out of here for a few hours."

"I can't leave the office in the middle of the day," I started to argue.

"Yes, you can. Text Edmund and lock the place up." She looked me up and down.

"Rowan—"

"By the way," she interrupted, "I love that gray color on you. Somehow, you make that maxi dress seem pretty. On anybody else it'd appear positively Amish."

Her rapid shift in conversation didn't faze me. "Well *I* like this dress."

"You should, it's flowing and romantic, plus it makes your eyes even more blue." She tapped a finger against her lips as she considered me. "You should have used that to your advantage against Mr. Walker."

I scoffed at the idea. "I appreciate the invite to lunch, but I really shouldn't leave."

"Oh yes, you should." Rowan tossed her head. "That, and I simply refuse to take no for an answer."

"Fine, fine." I gave in. "Let me grab my purse—shit," I said.

"What?"

"He's coming back in." I blew out a frustrated breath as he walked into the agency.

"You leave him to me," Rowan said, and when she turned around her whole stance had changed. "Well, hello," she purred.

"Hello there," Henry said, and flashed a very slow, masculine smile.

"Hannah and I are going out for lunch," she said in her low voice, and I felt the temperature shift in the office. She stepped over to Henry, projecting her power out. She reached up and trailed a hand down the side of his face.

In response, Henry didn't move a muscle.

"Jeez, Rowan." I shook my head at her maneuver.

"Sweet dreams, handsome," she said, and flashed a devastating smile. With a little hum, she stepped back from Henry and looped her arm through mine.

We walked out arm in arm while a dazed Henry continued to stare at the spot where Rowan had stood.

"You didn't fry his brain, did you?" I asked my cousin.

"Nope, I merely distracted him and kept his mind busy with a harmless little fantasy."

"Shameless." I smirked at her.

Rowan slipped her sunglasses on. "He'll snap out of it in a few minutes."

I tried very hard to appear stern. I failed, and tucked my tongue in my cheek instead. "Is it going to have any side-effects?"

"Other than a raging hard on?" Rowan wiggled her eyebrows at me. "No, not at all."

"Well here's hoping *that* effect has worn off when I get back from lunch," I said tartly.

"If not, use it to your advantage," Rowan suggested.

"That's practically Machiavellian." I shook my head.

"No, it's *smart*." Unrepentant, she grinned. "Men can't think past a hard on sweetie. First rule: 'Distract and deflect,' then 'charm and confuse'."

"I know, I know..." I muttered.

"He's an attractive man, and *distracting* him would be a hell of a lot more ethical than spelling him into forgetting what he knows."

"I'm not really comfortable with that either. I'd rather break out the magicks if it became necessary."

"Well seducing him into forgetting would be a lot more fun." Rowan gave me a playful jab with her elbow.

"Too bad I'm way out of practice."

Rowan's eyes grew wide. "Seriously? Honey when *was* the last time you got laid?"

"Maybe you could say that a little louder, cousin. I don't think the people across the street heard you."

In response, my cousin threw back her head and let loose a cackle like the Witch she was.

***

I did something I never did. I had drinks during work hours. Our lunch had consisted of appetizers and a couple of chocolate martinis. Feeling very relaxed, I gave my cousin a hug goodbye and walked the short distance back to the office a few hours later.

Henry was out, but I soon discovered that Edmund had been waiting for me. He pounced as soon as I shut the door, and started to lecture me about putting myself at risk the day before.

"It was my mother," I interrupted him. "Would you have done any less for yours?"

Edmund opened his mouth to argue, then shut it.

"We have a bigger problem at the moment." I sat in my desk chair and briefly explained to Edmund the interrogation I'd faced that morning.

"Shit," Edmund said, and began to pace.

"Exactly." I nodded. "When Rowan dropped by to check on me I took her up on her offer of lunch."

"I got your text as I was pulling in the parking lot." Edmund ran a hand through his hair. "Imagine my surprise when I walked in and found Henry staring off into space."

"He was lucky Rowan was in a playful mood."

"Sweet tap-dancing Christ on a pogo stick!" Edmund took in a deep breath and tried for composure. "I'm gonna strangle Rowan, the very next time I see her."

"All things considered, he got off easy," I reminded Edmund. "You know there are traditionally three options when an outsider stumbles across my family's talents, or starts making accusations."

"I know, I know…" Edmund shut his eyes. "Deflect and distract. Charm your way out of the situation, or—"

"Or go for the big guns and lay a magickal smack-down on the accuser," I finished.

"*Smack down*?" Edmund's eyes were round. "Sweetie, how much did you have to drink?"

I put my shoulders back. "I only had two martinis. I am *not* intoxicated."

"I'll try and run some interference for you with Henry," Edmund volunteered.

"You can try." I shrugged. "It's up to Mr. Walker whether or not he chooses to let this go on his own, or if I end up *encouraging* him to."

"Whoa, black magick woman." Edmund grinned.

"That's not funny," I snapped. "You know I'd move heaven and earth before I resorted to casting a major spell against someone." *Or used my sexuality as a weapon,* I thought. Even though Rowan had suggested it, that was a line I really didn't want to cross. Not ever.

Feeling miserable at the prospect, I forced myself to focus on the business at hand. The rest of the afternoon passed slowly. Edmund had a hot date, and I promised I would stay and lock up.

"I'm expecting a delivery around four o'clock," he said for the third time. "The new hard drive for my computer."

"I know. When it arrives I'll take it upstairs and put it in your apartment."

"Thanks, I appreciate it." He stopped, spun, and held out his arms. "How do I look?" he demanded.

"Hot," I said, admiring the dark slacks and crimson dress shirt he'd left unbuttoned at the throat. "So is this the third or fourth date?" I asked.

"Third," he answered, distracted as his date pulled up out front. I watched the tall, blonde man park his car. Edmund whistled appreciatively as his gorgeous date smiled and waved at us from the driver's seat. "I'm going after that like the rent is due, *tonight*," he said.

"Have fun." I grinned. "Play safe."

Edmund dropped a casual kiss on my cheek and was out the door. I felt a little maternal as I watched them drive away.

Edmund's computer part arrived right before closing, so as soon as I had everything shut down and locked up, I hitched my purse over my shoulder, and carried the box up the stairs. Fishing my key chain out of my bag, I let myself in Edmund's front door.

Package delivered, I was re-locking his apartment door when the scent of the harbor rolled over me, and goose bumps rose on my arms. "Hello Henry," I said, and braced myself for another confrontation.

I felt his hand on my shoulder and he turned me around to face him. He searched my eyes, as if by staring long enough, the answers he'd demanded earlier would somehow be there. "What is it about you?" he asked softly.

I inhaled and got hit with a new scent: patchouli and musk. What I detected wasn't his aftershave, it was a clairolfactory experience. The scent was earthy and rich, and it had my heart slamming in my throat. For me this fragrance meant one very specific thing: *Sexual desire.* As in his—for me. I was a little alarmed, because the desire was already in play naturally, and *not* as a result of any casting I'd done.

I gulped. "What do you need, Henry?" I heard myself say, and had a second to think that it was probably the stupidest phrase I could have uttered.

"Answers," he said, reaching out. He sank a hand in my hair, slid his fingers back and cupped the base of my head. Slowly, deliberately, he pulled me up to him, allowing me plenty of time to pull away—or to say no.

I didn't.

Our eyes locked, held, and his stayed open as he pressed his lips to mine. Captivated, I stared up at his bright green eyes. He kissed me again, catching my bottom lip with a softer kiss and I trembled.

I tipped my head back and my eyes drifted closed. This time when he lowered his mouth, his tongue teased my lips open. With a sigh, I rested my hands against his chest as our tongues met and we tasted each other. His other arm came out and pulled me close.

It had been a long, long time since I'd been held, or kissed so thoroughly by a man. I responded to those kisses without a thought, and part of me rejoiced in discovering that my sexuality wasn't dormant after all.

Suddenly he released his grip on my waist, and Henry lifted his head. My eyes fluttered open, and the expression on his face had me taking a step backwards. His brows were lowered, his mouth was set—hardly the appearance of a man caught up in the passion of the moment.

Neither of us said a word, but there was something in his eyes that let me know, while I may have enjoyed our kiss, he'd had other motives involved. Yes, he was attracted, but this had been a power play—plain and simple. A way for him to see if I'd crack under pressure and probably a way to take out some of the frustration Rowan's magick had stirred up.

I searched for my voice, and it took me a moment. "If you've quite finished."

I pulled my head back even though his hand was still in my hair. He opened his hand, and let the strands run through his fingers as I eased further away. I reached blindly for the railing. I eased down the first step, my eyes never leaving his.

He stayed where he was, watching me. "Go ahead and run," he said softly. "I'll still figure out what ever it is that you're hiding."

"I'm going home," I said moving down another step. "I'm not running."

He crossed his arms over his chest. "Keep telling yourself that, darlin'."

CHAPTER SEVEN

Some Witch I turned out to be. I'd been out maneuvered by a mundane.

He'd cast those sexual lures out there—and like some breathless neophyte, or inexperienced virgin, I'd fallen under his spell and had never even considered the possibility that he was playing me.

It was galling.

I'd been so caught up in the kiss that I never imagined he'd try and use *his* sexuality as a weapon against *me*—in order to get the information *he* wanted. No magick required.

And here I'd been worrying about crossing a line and being unethical...and that sonofabitch had managed to stir me up, make me feel stupid, and piss me off in record time.

I got through my evening, and even played Pirates with Eli. Tonight he'd been all about hidden treasure, and insisted that we search the apartment and even the gardens for the pieces of eight. By the time I'd put the bathroom back to rights after his bath, I was wiped out.

I tossed a night shirt on. I staggered to bed, plugged my phone in to charge on the nightstand, and lay there staring at the dark ceiling, restless and unable to sleep. I went over the day's events in my mind again and again. Frustrated, I rolled over to my side and saw a soft green glowing light coming from the nightstand drawer.

"The ring," I whispered.

I gently pulled the drawer open and patted around for the carved wooden box. I pulled it free and the light seemed to be leaking out from the hinged lid. *What had mom said?* I tried to recall. *That the poesy ring would make its magick known to me?* Apparently it was doing so right now.

I lifted the lid and the light seemed to coalesce, as if a little aura of light wrapped around the ring—only to sink into the jewel. The glow faded out as I watched. I took a breath and braced myself, wondering what would happen when I put it on this time.

I slipped the ring on my finger and it lay quietly. Almost disappointed that nothing had happened, I pulled it off and picked up my cell phone and shined its light on the interior of the band to study the engraving.

I'd had time to translate the Gaelic inscription. I knew what it meant now. "Pulse of my heart," I said.

The ring seemed unimpressed with my translation to English. I clicked off the flashlight app and set the phone aside. "Hmm...the last time I'd held the ring, I'd read the inscription out loud. Could that have been the catalyst?" I wondered. *"Cuirle mo croide,"* I said, letting it slip back on my third finger.

Then everything changed.

Like the first time the magick of the poesy ring had been activated, I began to experience another vision. While one reality slid over another, I stayed very still and waited to see what I would be shown this time.

The first thing I observed were my own hands as they ran across a broad masculine chest sprinkled with crisp hair. I heard myself sigh in appreciation at the firm muscles beneath my fingertips. *I knew this man.* He was the same one from the first vision. I watched my own nails rake lightly across his chest, as the jewel on my hand glowed with a bright, green light. The man shuddered in reaction at my explorations, and I was rolled from my side to my back.

My hands slid up his chest and I was nipping at the side of his neck, when he pulled my legs up higher. I gasped as the man slid inside me, his thrusts slow and deep. In response, I wrapped my arms and legs around him and hung on.

The man tangled his hands in my hair. "Damn it, I love you," he growled in my ear.

His words thrilled me. "I love you too," I whispered, kissing my way down his neck, and across the tattoo that was on his upper right shoulder. As I sampled that strong shoulder, I saw that the tattoo was all done in black...the design a ragged flag displaying a skull with two crossed swords beneath it.

The Jolly Roger.

Startled, I pulled back—intent on seeing the man's face—and then crazily I heard my grandmother's voice in my head. *Watch for the Pirate, Hannah.*

Like a bucket of ice water, my grandmother's voice slapped me out of the sexy vision quicker than anything else could have. I came back to the here and now. Flat on my back, panting and churned up, I yanked the ring off my finger immediately, dropping it to the tangled sheets.

"Bad timing, Grandma," I grumbled, sitting up. "Really bad...and I still didn't see his face!" Frustrated and churned up I scrubbed my hands over my own face. My skin was overheated, hyper sensitive and I felt like I had an overabundance of caffeine in my system.

Using the sheet so I wouldn't make skin contact with the ring, I gingerly picked it up. "By the goddess, I've had about enough of this." I dropped it back in the box and put it in my drawer. I was stomping off to take a cold shower when a part of the vision flashed back through my mind.

I stopped and grabbed for the doorframe to steady myself. "He told me that he loved me." I realized. *Well okay, technically, he'd said 'Damn it, I love you'.*

"And I responded with 'I love you, too'." I rubbed the heel of my hand over my heart. *How could a vision tap into my emotions?* I caught my reflection in the mirror over my dresser. My hair was sticking up, all tousled—almost as if someone had had their hands in it.

I gulped as a sudden fear rolled over me.

Had that been a vision, or a visit from some phantom lover? "I might have to ward the apartment from ghosts if this keeps up," I told myself.

And why hadn't I seen his face? I knew his body, how it felt, how it tasted...and now I knew he had a tattoo. A pirate flag tattoo. My mind raced with possibilities: past life memories, a haunting, or maybe the ring was possessed. I broke into a nervous sweat thinking about it.

Wide awake and more than a little concerned, I went to the bathroom and stripped off. With a yank I had water pouring out of the shower, and I stepped under the spray, bracing my hands on the tile as the water sluiced over my head. *Maybe a nice cool shower would help.*

It really didn't help.

***

I had a very long, completely sleepless night. But I'd put the time to good use and hit the internet. I'd researched the Jolly Roger, pirate flags in general, also clairvoyant visions, past life memories, and spirit possession. Good news? I had ruled out possession. Neither I nor the ring were possessed. Call it Witch's intuition, but I was absolutely certain that my grandmother would never leave me anything remotely dangerous or harmful.

More than likely the emerald was simply doing what it was rumored to...giving me a glimpse of my future lover. And 'glimpse' was accurate. As I still hadn't seen the man's face, only a pirate tattoo. As I dressed for the day I decided to take my grandmother's advice to heart—and keep watch. I slipped on the sky blue summer dress again, and a pair of espadrille wedges, in tan.

In defiance, I pulled a favorite silver pendant out of my jewelry box. The pendant featured an open butterfly design with a small pentacle at its center. On top of the pentacle an amethyst was centered. It was subtle, and difficult to see the pentacle design unless you were very close to the pendant.

I attached it to a long chain, slipped it on, and checked to make sure that only the top of the butterfly wings were visible. Still, the magickal pendant made me feel better, and *empowered*. I'd need that today. I still had to face down Henry Walker, and the vision the night before had totally distracted me from worrying over that embarrassing scenario yesterday afternoon.

If Henry Walker thought I'd be easily susceptible to that good looking, bad boy routine...he was sadly mistaken. I'd show him. This Witch could more than hold her own against some slow-talking mundane. No matter how charming he tried to be.

Not that he was charming. Not in any way.

I checked my reflection. My hair waved around my face, and the blue dress made my eyes brighten up, or maybe that was simply righteous indignation. I deliberately deepened my eye shadow, added a touch more eyeliner, and sprayed on some lilac body spray.

I could handle Henry Walker. I nodded to myself. *Besides, I had a mystery to solve. I needed to figure out who the man was from the visions.* Strangely I was starting to develop feelings for that mystery lover… whoever he was. *Because great goddess if he was half as talented between the sheets in real life, as he was in the visions, the man was a keeper.*

I slid some mauve lipstick on. "Now all I have to do," I said to my reflection, "is conjure up a way to casually ask every nicely built man in town between the ages of twenty-five and forty, to strip off their shirts and show me their tattoos."

Sure, Hannah. I mentally rolled my eyes at that.

A nasty thunderstorm had begun to brew. The clouds rolled heavy from the west, and the air was thick and dense. Thunder rumbled, and when I dropped Eli off at daycare the sky had a slightly green cast to it. While the guy on the radio warned of severe thunderstorms within the hour, I glanced at the sky and tossed my head. *Bring it on,* I thought.

I loved a good summer storm, and today the weather seemed to match my mood perfectly: Frustrated, on edge, with a touch of mean. I slammed my car door and marched to the office. My cell phone buzzed and I discovered a text from Edmund. Apparently he'd gotten lucky last night and was spending the morning with his boyfriend. He'd be in after noon.

"Perfect," I said through gritted teeth. "That way when I zap that egotistical Henry Walker to a crisp, they'll be no one around to witness me disposing of his body." A crack of thunder punctuated my words, and with a grim smile, I tucked the phone away, unlocked the door and let myself in the office.

I hit the lights, went straight to the mini fridge and snagged a bottle of cold water. I thumped it down on my desk, tucked my purse away, and sat down. I booted up my computer, pulled out a notepad and began to play back the messages from the answering machine. I'd managed maybe twenty minutes of peace and quiet before I heard Henry amble down the stairs from his apartment.

The temper I'd tried to keep at bay began to boil as soon as I heard those boots hit the hardwood floor. I set my jaw and did my best to ignore him. A gust of wind had our front door pushing in slightly from the difference in the pressure as the storm rolled closer.

Henry moved in my line of sight. "Hannah, do I have any messages?"

"Yes, you do." Without sparing him a glance, I snatched a stack of messages from the desk and snapped my hand up in the air. "If you'd be so kind as to return them."

"I'll get right on that, this morning," he drawled, taking the notes.

"That," I said acidly, "would be a refreshing change."

"Something sure has you riled up." Henry leaned a hip on my desk. I could see him out of my peripheral vision. My shoulders stiffened when he smiled down at me.

He was baiting me. I knew it, and still I couldn't help but snarl at him. "Get your ass off my desk."

He started to laugh. "I don't think I've ever hear you cuss before."

I kept working on the computer, and refused to spare him a glance. "Be assured Mr. Walker, the very last thing you want—is for me to curse you."

In response to my words, a gust of wind pushed against the office and the front door slammed open, bouncing off the wall. Several file folders blew off my desk and I jumped up to grab them. Henry got up to close the door, flipping the lock so it wouldn't blow open again. I knelt down to gather up the files and papers.

"Let me give you a hand." Henry crouched down next to me and reached for a file.

"I've got them," I said, pushing the files together. I jolted when I felt his hand on my arm.

"Here, darlin'."

I shrugged his hand off, rejecting his assistance. "No thank you," I said, rocking back on my heels and rising up. I brushed at my dress and went directly to my desk to begin to put the files in order.

Henry dropped a file on top of the ones I was attempting to reorganize. With a hiss of impatience I shoved it aside. I was opening my mouth to tell him to leave the files alone, when the storm broke.

Lightning flashed and thunder boomed. The sky was so dark, it was as if night had fallen. Rain pelted down and I heard a tinny sound. I stepped to the front windows in time to see a hailstone ricochet off the ground. First a couple, then dozens began to bounce off the sidewalk out front. They morphed quickly from pea-size to bigger than quarters. The noise was incredible.

"Shit," I said, worrying of possible hail damage to my car. I searched out with my powers. *Element of air,* I sent out silently, *is there any real danger?* The information was sent back to me swiftly. *The storm would subside without any major damage. But for the next half hour it was going to put on a hell of a show.*

A simultaneous explosion of lightning and thunder shook the building and the power went out. The strike had been close by. The office went pitch black, and Henry yanked me away from the windows.

"Get away from there!" he said, pulling me across the floor.

"Hey, hands off!" I smacked his hand off my arm.

"Damn it, Hannah," Henry snarled, dropping his hand.

"Are you incapable of comprehending acceptable social niceties, or even professional workplace behavior?" I yelled over the storm.

Thunder shook the building as Henry got up in my

face. "Do you have trouble understanding that you need to stay away from windows during a severe storm?"

My mood aligned itself to the storm, and furious, I got right up in his face as well. "If you put your hands on me one more time, you'll regret it!"

The wind howled and the glass rattled in the panes. "Is there a basement?" he shouted over the storm.

I rolled my eyes at him. "It's only a thunderstorm. The wind is simply having a tantrum."

"Sounds like someone else I know," Henry said, and with that, he grabbed my arm and hauled me into his office.

I fought him the whole way. But my soles on my shoes were slick and I slid across the floor as if it were an ice rink. He shoved me inside his windowless office and slammed the door behind us. "Listen sister. You and me, we need to have a talk."

Glancing at his desk, I picked up the first thing I saw. I spun around and threw his coffee mug straight at his head. "Who the hell do you think you are?"

He ducked and the mug shattered against the wall behind him. He reached out, grabbed me by the arms. "Knock it off!" he said, yanking me up to my toes.

I struggled and tried to kick at him, all that got me was pulled up tight to his chest. My breath whooshed out when our chests rapped together.

"Get your hands off me," I managed.

"You *like* my hands on you." To prove his point he ran them down my back.

"I most certainly do not!"

He leaned down, until we were nose to nose. "Yeah, you do. Admit it."

I grabbed ahold of his shirt. "You *arrogant* motherfu—"

He cut off my words by grinding his mouth down on mine. For a few seconds I kept my mouth clamped shut. Then he slid his hands up, running them gently through my hair.

That tender touch in contrast to the rough kiss had me gasping in surprise. Henry took immediate advantage of that and his tongue swept in and claimed my mouth.

All the anger I'd built up from the maneuver he'd pulled the day before combined with the sexual frustration of that last vision, detonated in my system. The energetic and emotional blast was so loud that I felt the ground shake.

The storm continued to crash over the building, and furious, frustrated and turned on—I kissed him back, every bit as hard as he was kissing me.

I let go of his shirt and grabbed ahold of his tousled hair and pulled his head down farther to mine. He responded by bending me backwards over his arm. Now his hands were racing over me, and I trembled when I felt him pass his hand over my breast. When he gave the peak of my breast a little tweak, I moaned in response.

I heard a different crashing sound and the next thing

I knew my back hit the now cleared desk. Henry's hands were under my dress touching, and teasing, and I gnawed on his mouth. In the back of my mind, I knew we were racing towards the point of no return. And the rest of me didn't give a damn. I ran my hands over him, as desperate to touch him as I was to be touched.

Cerebral, thoughtful Hannah was floating away and leaving earthy, ravenous Hannah to her desires. I didn't know this Hannah, but a part of me rejoiced in letting her loose. I tugged his shirt free of his jeans, heard it tear, and laughed.

I felt him yank my panties down my legs, and he lifted his mouth from mine, shoved my dress up and out of the way, and began to kiss his way down my chest towards my belly, and lower. My back arched off the desk and I screamed when he tasted me. He pushed my legs apart and buried his face between them.

Dream lovers aside, it had been far too long, and I was shouting from an orgasm within moments. While the thunderstorm raged, I lay dazed and blinking at the ceiling, trying to get my breath back. Belatedly, I heard him unbuckle and unzip and before I could even begin to process the fact that Henry Walker had just gone down on me, I felt his calloused hands on my hips, and he pressed forward.

I hissed at the surprising sting of his penetration. He was large, and I was stretched to the point of pain.

"Shit, Hannah." Henry leaned over. "Darlin' you're really tight." I heard a whimper, and wondered who'd made that sound.

"Take a breath Hannah," Henry suggested and eased back a little.

I gasped and ran my hands down his arms, and tried to relearn how to breathe. My eyes locked on his, and I took a deep breath in and let it out slowly.

"Do you want me to stop?"

"No," I shook my head, and noticed that while his jaw was set, his arms were trembling from holding back. For some reason, that alone helped me relax. I concentrated on making my muscles unclench. As soon as they did, the discomfort eased up. I blew out a shaky breath.

"Are you okay?" he asked while the rain and hail pounded down over the building.

I moved experimentally beneath him, and watched him shudder. "I'm fine," I said firmly.

"Hannah," he began.

To shut him up, I pressed a hard, quick kiss to his mouth.

He smiled down at me, and the glint in his eyes had me gasping. Slowly, he pushed his way forward.

"*Shit!*" I said, not in pain—but pleasure.

Henry lowered his mouth, kissed me long and deep, and began to move. Carefully at first, but when I reached around and grabbed his back side, he got the message and began to thrust harder and faster. The desk made a horrible racket as it scooted across the floor, and I was starting to build up to another orgasm when

Henry threw his head back and was shouting with his own release.

He dropped down on top of me, and the thunder gave a half hearted rumble, and rolled away. Not unlike the second climax I'd been building up to. The hail was gone now, and only rain beat against the roof.

After a few moments Henry sighed and lifted his weight off me. He stepped back and my eyes widened when I saw that he'd been wearing a condom.

Efficiently he dealt with it, and my stomach gave a nasty pitch when I realized that I'd been too far gone to even stop and think about protection. *That should never have happened.*

None of this should've happened. I corrected myself.

I started to sit up, and Henry tugged me to a sitting position. I recalled the state of my dress a bit too late and hurriedly yanked it down.

"Well," he said with a cheerful grin as he zipped back up. "That was fun."

"*Fun?*" Offended, I scowled at him.

"You gonna look me in the eye, and tell me you didn't have fun?" He reached out and tucked my hair behind my ear. "Darlin' you were shouting down the walls."

Incredibly insulted, I opened my mouth to scream at him and found that for once I didn't have any words. I stood up, wobbled and caught myself on the desk. The lights chose that exact moment to come back on. I spotted my underwear lying on the floor. They'd landed at the bottom of the door.

I held my head up and walked to the door, stopping only to grab my underwear, then I threw the door open with enough force that it bounced off the wall. I went directly to the bathroom, locked the door behind me and leaned against it.

Oh my gods! What had I done?

I'd gotten into a fight with Henry and had sex! I covered my face with my hands and groaned. *I didn't even like him! He was abrasive and annoying and I'd...I'd...what was the phrase Edmund had used?*

Gone after him like the rent was due tonight.

Appalled at my behavior, I gave into the shakes and eventually forced myself to go to the sink, wash up and put my underwear back on...which was humiliating in the extreme.

I flashed back to him zipping up and grinning at me, "*Well, that was fun.*" he'd said, and that Southern twang echoed horribly in my mind.

I frowned hard at the woman staring back at me from the mirror. Her hair was a wreck, the pretty sky blue dress was wrinkled, her face was very pale, and eyes were huge. "What have you done?" I asked my reflection.

I shut my eyes for a moment and gripped the counter. "Oh shit," I whispered, and identified the emotion I was feeling as shame. I stayed where I was, playing everything back in my mind, and came to the realization that the whole thing had made me feel—

cheap.

I opened my eyes and faced the truth, which was that I couldn't hide forever. So, I dried my hands, smoothed my hair and psyched myself up to exit the bathroom. I opened the door, walked back into the main office and was shocked to discover that Henry was no where to be seen.

"Well," I said to the empty office. "At least he didn't leave money on the desk for services rendered." Hearing my own words out loud made me cringe a bit, and weirdly I felt like crying.

Face it girl, my inner monologue chastised. *You acted cheap and easy and that's exactly the way you got treated.* I gulped against the nausea that churned through me. All I wanted now was to get out of there. I was absolutely mortified.

I yanked my purse out of the desk and ran.

CHAPTER EIGHT

I drove to my favorite beach. I slipped my sunglasses on, kicked off my shoes and walked in the surf for a while thinking things over. The wind coming off the water helped, and I found a little peace in the embrace of my element. Carefully, I made my way over the cobbles and found a boulder to sit on. Now that the storm was over, the heat had lessened, and the wind coming off the ocean was crisp and bracing.

I tossed my head, faced the wind, and allowed the conflicting emotions I was experiencing to work their way out of my system.

First I had to work my way past the humiliation that I'd actually had sex in the office, with a man I was admittedly attracted to—but who I didn't even particularly like.

I wasn't the casual sex type. Never had been. Yet look what had happened.

Second, and this nasty thought had kicked in on the drive to the secluded beach—he'd used a condom.

While I was relieved that he'd been smart enough to do so...it also meant that he'd either had one in his pocket, or gods help me maybe in his desk drawer just in case he got lucky. Which made me feel doubly played.

Because he'd been *prepared*. As in planning ahead.

And finally...I kind of felt like I'd cheated on that lover from my visions. It was slightly ridiculous feeling that way, but there you were. Unbidden, the final line from the charm of the poesy ring came to mind: *"To a steadfast soul the legacy passes, heavy though it may be, to become bewitched and beloved, blessed by the moon, stars, and sea."*

I definitely had the bewitched part down, but I was no one's beloved. Henry didn't love me. We'd both...*had an itch,* I supposed. *And we'd scratched it.* It wasn't too pretty when you put it that way—yet the truth often wasn't.

In real life, I doubted anyone could compete with the sensual skills of the mystery man from the visions. That man had been an incredible lover, one who'd both thrilled and given me an amazing amount of pleasure. While today's fiasco had been more of a 'wham-bam-thank-you-ma'am' type of scenario.

If I closed my eyes, I could remember perfectly the feel of that mystery lover's mustache across the nape of my neck and the texture of his hands on my bare skin. I could still clearly see that gorgeous chest from the night before, and the pirate flag tattoo. I'd never even seen his face, but I knew the taste of his bare skin and somehow...I *was* connected to him.

Whoever he was.

The term 'soul mate' wasn't one I was comfortable with. It had been used to death thanks to the New Agers, but I was beginning to wonder: *was the man the poesy ring had shown me glimpses of, my soul mate?*

"Well then, where are you?" I asked the wind.

There was no answer, so I wrapped my arms around my knees and gazed out to the sea.

***

I stayed for a few hours letting the elements of water and air comfort me. I drove back to town and picked up Eli from daycare. I purposefully ignored my cell phone, and it wasn't until I was halfway home that I remembered the pool party we'd been invited to.

My sister and her husband threw an elaborate pool party at their home every year right before the first harvest, the festival of Lughnasadh. My entire family attended, as well as Kayleigh and Curtis' friends and neighbors. It was the last thing I wanted to do, yet Eli had been so excited about the pool party. So I sucked it up, put on a happy face for my son, and decided to go anyway.

I showered when I got home, and chose my outfit carefully. Dark denim shorts, a black cami with a long, lacy, sleeveless top over that. I strapped on some metallic sandals, brushed my hair in a high ponytail, and redid my makeup. Because I was in a mood, I went for dramatic eye color and deep charcoal liner. I rummaged through my makeup, wondering which lipstick to use. I held up a dark red tube, one that Edmund had bought for me, but I'd never had the guts to wear. And went ahead and put that one on.

"You're pretty, Mama." Eli sat on the side of the bathtub, swinging his feet.

"Thanks, baby." I put the cosmetics away.

"Let's go, let's go!" Eli grabbed my hand and tugged me towards the door.

I could smell the barbeque as soon as we parked on the street. I hauled a large tote bag that carried my purse, phone and Eli's towel, and took Eli's hand firmly in mine. We walked around the back of my sister's spacious home to the gate.

"Remember the pool rules," I said to Eli.

Eli grinned up at me, wearing red swim trunks, a white tank, and his blue pool goggles. "I can swim. I swim real good," he argued.

"Yes, I know you can," I said opening the gate. "However you will stay in the shallow end of the pool or you won't go in at all."

Eli's bottom lip poked out. "Okay," he grumbled.

I heard my name called, and I lifted a hand in greeting. Eli made a mad dash for the in-ground pool. He tossed his tank top down, kicked off his flip-flops and waded in the water, heading straight for his cousin Margot.

I went directly to a chair at the shady side of the pool, settled in and kept watch over my son. I told myself I wouldn't brood over the day's events. Yet I started to anyway.

"Hey, Hannah." Rowan sat beside me wearing a red bikini top and denim shorts. "Girl, you look good."

"Thanks," I said distractedly, accepting the frozen Margarita she handed me.

"No seriously," Rowan said, sipping at her drink. "Something put you in a mood, and you wear it well."

To my surprise I discovered I wanted to confide in her badly, but sitting in Kayleigh's backyard surrounded by splashing children, our witchy family, and my sister's mundane neighbors was hardly the place for that type of conversation. "Rowan, I—" I caught myself, shook my head and sipped at the drink before the words started to tumble out.

I heard my mother call out that dinner would be ready in five minutes and she waved me over to help. I told Eli to climb out of the pool to dry off, and when Rowan volunteered to stay and keep and eye on him, I got up and went to give my mother and sister a hand.

Kayleigh and I were carrying out food to the covered patio when a scent caught my attention. I recognized it immediately. It was the same one that I'd detected right before I'd seen Henry Walker for the first time. The scent of brine, water and the beach.

I took a deep breath, forced myself to step outside, and discovered Henry Walker was indeed at my sister's home, and he was wearing new clothes. A thin, blue plaid shirt, and dark denim shorts were casual but stylish and unwrinkled. He was holding a bottle of beer and chatting easily with my father and Edmund. I was so surprised to see him that I stopped in my tracks and bobbled the pasta salad.

Kayleigh walked right into me. "Hannah!" she laughed.

"Sorry." I shook off my shock, while my sister called out a cheery hello to both Henry and Edmund. *What the hell? How did Kayleigh know him?*

Henry's eyes locked on mine. Slowly he inclined his head in acknowledgment.

I slapped the bowl down on the long table with a bit more force than necessary. Grabbing my sister by the elbow, I steered her inside. "What's that man doing here?" I hissed.

"Curtis and I invited him," Kayleigh said.

"How do you know him?"

"Curtis is his real estate agent," she said. "He showed him a piece of property on the outskirts of town. Henry put an offer on it this afternoon."

"Oh," I managed. "I didn't know."

"I thought Edmund would have told you," Kayleigh said, prying my hand loose. "The man has a better line on gossip than I do."

"Well, why did you invite him here?" I asked, again.

Kayleigh rolled her eyes. "He's new in town, your business partner, and an old friend of Edmund's."

"He's *not* my partner—"

"We thought he would enjoy himself," Kayleigh interrupted.

My mother walked in oblivious to the conversation. "What are you girls doing in here? Let's go out and eat." She shooed us along.

I put on a false smile and joined the family at the tables. As luck would have it, Rowan and Margot were seated across from me. Eli was to my right and Edmund sat down to my left. Henry was on the opposite side of Edmund, so I focused my attention on my cousin, Edmund and the children and tried to ignore Henry.

I probably shouldn't have bothered. Kayleigh was trying so hard to keep Henry's attention that if I wouldn't have known any better, I'd have said she was flirting. But more likely she was trying to pump him for information, so she'd have something to gossip about.

I managed to make it through dinner, thanks mostly to Rowan and the children. Afterwards I went back to my poolside chair, while my sister slipped inside to feed the baby, and kept an eye on Eli and Margot as they played *Marco Polo* with a few other children in the water.

I jolted when a bottle of beer was set on the little table at my side. "Brought you a drink." Henry took a seat next to me.

"I don't drink beer," I said, and angled my head slightly away from him. *Damn it! I'd done my best to avoid him for hours,* I thought. *And now the man plops himself down next to me as if nothing ever happened between the two of us.* I caught a hint of the ocean, sitting next to him. The tang of seawater and crazily the scent of the little rocky beach I'd visited earlier today.

He smelled like one of my favorite places... I realized while my stomach clenched, and my heart began to beat a little faster. I'd had strong reactions to people in the past, thanks to my weird psychic ability, but, *damn*. This was hitting a new all time, embarrassing high. I breathed through my mouth and tried not to notice that Henry looked even better close up in that new shirt and denim shorts. He shifted in his chair, our shoulders brushed, and I felt a little bead of sweat run down my back.

"I want to talk to you," Henry began.

"Not here," I said.

"No one will overhear us. The kids are making too much noise." As if to back up his words, two older children did cannonballs into the deep end of the pool. A smattering of applause broke out from the party goers. "Why did you take off this morning?" he wanted to know.

"Me?" I whipped my head around to glare at him. "You were the one who had disappeared after I came out of the restroom."

"I went upstairs for a second, I'd been waiting for you, but when I came back, you'd high-tailed it out of there."

"High-tailed?" I tossed my head. "What a charming

Southern colloquialism."

"Don't play the bitch card with me, Hannah."

I slowly turned my head to stare at him. "Excuse me?"

"You take that snotty tone every time you hear something you don't like. What happened today was—"

"Mr. Walker," I cut him off. "As far as I'm concerned today was a mistake, a *huge* mistake. One that I have no intention of ever repeating."

"Mistake?" Henry's voice lowered to a growl.

"Mama!" Eli shouted as he and Margot began to play sword fight with foam pool noodles. "Watch me. Watch me!"

"I'm watching," I called back.

"We had fun." Henry's voice was pitched low. "So what's your problem?"

I raised my eyebrows at him. "So you said earlier. I can't tell you how flattering it is to keep hearing that I *amused* you."

"You know what I meant." He laid his hand on mine where it rested on the arm of the pool chair. "I'm into you Hannah," Henry said. "Damned if I know why."

His gesture combined with the soft words made my insides quake. The unexpected tenderness, albeit gruff, simply killed me.

My parents walked up, and I saw my chance for escape. "Mom, Dad," I called over to them. "Would you keep an eye on Eli and Margot?"

"Sure thing, honey," my father said.

I walked away from Henry as quickly as possible, but not fast enough that it would seem like I was running. I went straight to the house, and hunted up my sister. I found her, alone in the baby's room, changing Madison.

"Hi!" I said brightly.

Kayleigh glanced over her shoulder. "What are you doing in here? You should be out there enjoying the party." She finished snapping the baby's onesie into place and picked her up.

The baby's room was painted a soft lavender. I caught an herbal scent and spotted a small vase of garden roses and lavender sprigs that had been placed on a tall dresser. Floral print curtains and coordinating linens decorated the baby's room, which fit my herbalist sister, right down to the ground.

I went in and took the baby. "I *am* enjoying myself. I came in here to hang out with two of my favorite Witches." I kissed Maddie's soft cheek. "This is such a pretty nursery, Kayleigh."

"You're the one that found the fabric for the curtains," she said, going to the adjoining bathroom. "Is there something going on with you and Henry Walker?" Kayleigh asked while she washed her hands.

"No!" I scoffed, and the sound caused the baby startle. I started to pat and sway, trying to soothe my niece.

"Umm hmm." Kayleigh came back out, rolling her eyes at me. "He's been staring at you all evening."

"He has not."

"Come on." She put an arm around me. "Let's go downstairs and rejoin the party."

We'd taken no more than a few steps when I stopped dead on her upper landing. A tingling started at the base of my neck and the acrid smell of smoke filled my nose. "Smoke," I said. "Kayleigh, something's burning."

Kayleigh gave me a squeeze. "The smoke detectors aren't going off. Are you receiving clairolfactory information?"

"Yeah." I shook my head as the scent grew stronger. "I smell gasoline too."

"Focus," Kayleigh said intently. "Hannah, hone in on that information. Find the fire."

I handed the baby back to my sister, and shut my eyes letting my body act as a compass. I felt a tug to my right and I spun to face the direction I felt pulled in. "It's deliberate, and being set right now." I heard myself say. "It's close. Across the street maybe," I said, opening my eyes.

Kayleigh nodded and we went down the stairs together. She opened the front door and checked outside. "I don't see anything," Kayleigh said.

"Whose house is that?" I pointed to the brick three story across the road.

"The Miller's," Kayleigh said. "They're here right now."

I focused on the attractive house with the deep blue shutters, and the next scent that hit me had me flinching. "Ozone," I said. "Kayleigh, call the fire department! Send them across the street to the Miller's house."

"I will!" Kayleigh said. "Go! See if you can stop it!"

I jogged across the street, pounded over the pretty manicured lawn and followed my nose. When my instincts told me to go around the left side of the house I didn't question, I simply ran faster. I saw the gate on the tall white vinyl privacy fence and pushed out with both hands. The gate flung itself wide open and I never broke stride. I rushed around to the back and discovered that the shed door was open. *Someone was inside.*

The odor of gasoline bloomed in the air, and smoke started to pour out of the shed door. "Hey!" I shouted, and a young man bolted out of the shed and started to run. He jumped up and scrambled over the top of the privacy fence so fast, I could only blink.

As I dashed towards the shed the stench of ozone hit me. *Get back!* my intuition screamed, and I skidded to a stop. To my surprise someone bumped solidly into me from behind. We both went down.

"Are you crazy?" Henry yanked me to my feet. "Did you at least get a good look at the kid?"

The combined stench of smoke, gasoline and ozone made my stomach heave. I grabbed Henry's shirt and pulled him a few steps farther away from the shed. "It's going to blow up!" I said.

"What's going to blow up?" He scowled at me. "The shed?"

"Trust me!" I yanked harder, as adrenalin coursed through me. "Come on!"

"For the love of god." Henry shook my grip from his shirt. "Hannah, calm down." He started going towards the shed.

There wasn't any time. He wasn't listening, I had only seconds to act. "I'm sorry about this," I said.

"What?" He paused in mid-step.

"I'm sorry, Henry." Pulling up my magick from my gut, I flung my hands out and aimed my power straight at him. Between my fear and the rush of adrenalin, the element of air instantly came to my call. It hit Henry straight in the solar plexus, knocking him off his feet, and back through the air, away from the shed a good twenty feet.

He went down hard, and I had barely enough time to drop to the grass myself. I managed to cover my head as the gasoline can inside the shed exploded, sending a whoosh of flames skyward, and shrapnel across the lawn.

I grunted when something heavy hit the back of my leg, and then after a few seconds, I lifted my head to check on Henry. He was lying flat on his back, and he wasn't moving.

I staggered to my feet and went to him as quickly as I could. I dropped down beside him. "Henry, can you hear me?" I panicked, and placed my ear to his chest trying to listen for a heart beat. I felt his chest rise up and down, and I ignored the sounds of the shouting in the background and the approaching sirens. *There. There it was.* I heard his heart beating and blew out a relieved breath.

I sat back up; my head began to spin, and my fingers went numb. I heard a loud buzzing sound in my ears. I tried to stand, managed a few steps, and the world began to tilt.

***

I frowned as I focused on the face that leaned over me. "Dad?" I asked, trying to make sense of everything. My nose burned, there was a terrible taste in my mouth, and the back of my leg hurt.

"I've got you," my father said as neighbors, my family, and the fire department poured around the side of the Miller's house.

I tried to sit up, and ended up tipping over against my father. "Ow!" I hissed in a breath, as pain began to radiate up my leg.

"Hannah, you took five years off my life." My father eased me back down. "Does anything hurt?"

"My right leg."

My father rotated my leg to the side. I craned my neck to see for myself, and discovered why my leg had been hurting. A nice gash was there, and the combination of seeing the injury, and the smell of fire and blood, made me feel light headed all over again.

"Shit!" I turned my face away and found that two

EMT's were crouched over Henry where he lay on the ground a few feet away. I swallowed hard. "Oh no," I whispered. *He still wasn't moving.*

"What happened?" My father asked.

I raised my eyes to his. "I saw the kid who set the fire. I could smell the gasoline and ozone...I knew it would go up." I kept my voice low. "I tried to warn Henry but he wouldn't listen, so I blew him out of harms way."

My father sighed. "He saw you call down your element?"

"He was looking straight at me." My voice shook. "I'm sorry Dad, there wasn't any time." *And I was sorry,* I thought. *Sorry to my ancestors who'd been persecuted, to my family who'd kept our legacy hidden, and especially to the man I'd knocked on his ass.*

My father pressed a kiss to the top of my head. "Don't worry about that right now."

"I hope I didn't hurt him," I whispered, as tears began to roll down my cheeks.

"Hush," my father soothed. "You probably saved his life." He motioned over to the EMTs. "Over here please, my daughter is hurt."

I wiped the tears away and tried to focus my attention on the EMT who'd begun assessing my injury.

There was a ruckus when Henry regained consciousness. It took a firefighter and two EMTs to keep him on the ground. "Hannah?" he called.

My heart lurched, hearing his voice. "I'm right

here." I reached out and patted his shoe.

"Are you alright?" Henry asked.

"Fine."

"Haven't been hit in the bread basket like that..." I heard him wheeze, "...since my days of college football."

I breathed a sigh of relief. *At least he was okay.*

The EMTs insisted that Henry go to hospital and get checked out in case he had a concussion. Henry gave in, *after* Edmund gave him grief, but Henry complained loudly over the ambulance. Then he insisted that I ride along as I was the one with a visible injury.

I refused, and instead my father drove me to the hospital. I ended up getting some stitches in the back of my leg. I gave my statement to the police, but my mind raced over everything that had happened in the past twenty-four hours.

The vision, Henry and I together at the office, the fire, me hitting him with magick...

Edmund checked in, said Henry was being released, and since he did have a mild concussion Edmund would be keeping an eye on him tonight. I was able to leave the ER a short time after, and when I arrived home Eli was sitting up on the couch curled up with my mother watching his favorite movie, *Pirates of the Caribbean*. He pounced on me as soon as I limped in, and it took a while to settle him down. Eventually, he fell asleep on my lap.

Mom bundled him off to bed, and I sat on the couch

with my leg propped up and resting on my father's lap.

Once Eli was down, my father wasted no time getting into specifics of the magick I'd done on Henry Walker.

"How hard did you hit him?" he wanted to know.

"Do you remember that time Nathan and I were playing soccer?" I asked.

"Oh Hannah, you didn't." My mother rolled her eyes to the ceiling. "I think this calls for a drink." At home, she got up to help herself to the wine in the fridge.

"You and your brother are the reason I went prematurely gray," my father announced.

I hunched my shoulders defensively. "I was only thirteen. I didn't have control over my abilities, and besides, he'd been calling me names."

"I'll never forget that day." He patted my knee. "You nailed your brother with a blast of air, sent him flying a good fifteen feet. It knocked Nathan out cold, sprained his wrist, *and* gave him a concussion."

"Well, I broke my distance record today."

"How far did he go?" he wanted to know.

"I'd guess around twenty feet," I said.

"*Really?*" My father laughed.

"Padrick!" My mother complained. "This is no laughing matter!"

While Dad continued to chuckle, my mother gave me the stink eye. "Hannah Osborne Pogue," she said, sounding pissed.

"I'd run out of options." I shifted on the couch,

trying to get comfortable. "If I wouldn't have blasted him away from the shed, he'd have been seriously injured, or maybe even killed."

"What's done is done," my father said. "You knocked him out after all, he may not even remember you calling upon your element."

"And if he does remember, Padrick?" Mom asked. "What then?"

"We'll convince him that he imagined it." Dad winked at me. "After all, he did get bumped in the head."

CHAPTER NINE

The next morning I was informed that I was to take the day off work, per Edmund's orders. Mom headed in to open the spice shop, and Dad took Eli to daycare for me so I would have some time alone. I puttered around the apartment with the cat for company, and I managed to take a bath by keeping my leg braced on the rim of the tub, and washed my hair in the kitchen sink.

I sat on the bed, slowly combed out the tangles and tried to figure out why I had all of these conflicting feelings regarding Henry Walker. It simply didn't add up. *How could one man cause me to be annoyed, attracted, charmed, and confused all at the same time?* I set the comb aside, pulled the carved box out, flipped up the hinge and stared at the poesy ring.

"It's all your fault," I grumbled. "Ever since I inherited you, I've been all twisted up inside...impulsive *and* reckless."

I twisted the box in my hand and watched the light catch the emerald. Unlike the sexy visions the poesy ring had granted, yesterday had hardly been the romantic fantasy of my dreams. We hadn't even completely undressed. And it was intense, frantic and over far too soon.

"Grow up Hannah," I sighed. "Stop comparing fantasy to reality. You may be a Witch, but your life isn't a faery tale." Without touching the ring, I shut the box, carefully tucking it away again.

I thought it over some more and brewed myself a cup of tea. *Maybe the ring had only shown me what I wanted to see? Shown me what was possible—but not actual?*

No matter what was happening in my personal life, the family's magickal legacy had to remain safely hidden. With that responsibility pressing on me, I pulled out my oldest magickal journals and spell books and reluctantly began putting together a spell—in case I would have to make Henry Walker forget the magick that he'd seen me do.

A few hours later, I sat at my kitchen table in my ratty gray shorts and a faded butterfly tank top. Surrounded by spells and incantations, I dropped my head in my hands. The prospect of working manipulative magick held little appeal, but after thinking everything over...I had to admit that adjusting his memories might be my only viable option.

A sharp knock at the door jolted me out of my brooding. "Hannah!" Rowan called, "Open up. I brought lunch!"

I limped over to the door and checked the clock, surprised that so much time had passed. I flipped the lock and held the door open for my gorgeous cousin. Rowan blew into the apartment in a long blood-red summer dress and with her tresses done in an intricate braid down her back.

"An offering to the local heroine!" Rowan laughed, pressing a kiss to my cheek.

"Thanks." I shut the door behind her.

"Hannah?" Rowan frowned. "Are you feeling bad?"

"No," I lied, brushing past her.

"You're schlepping around in your oldest clothes, and don't have any makeup on." Rowan was scandalized.

"Yeah, so? Who's going to see me?" I went to the table and began clearing away the books and notes.

It only took Rowan a couple of seconds to figure out what I'd been studying. "Uncle Padrick filled me in. Are you going to have to spell Henry Walker, after all?"

"I don't know yet," I admitted.

"Hey, honey, are you sure that you're okay?" Her face mirrored her concern. "You're putting out some intense vibes."

"I'm fine. I just embarrassed myself at work yesterday, that's all." I cleared off the books, gathered up my notes.

"That guy, Henry?" Rowan pulled the sub sandwiches out. "Now that I've had a chance to check him out, I have to admit. He's pretty hot."

"You think so?" I said. "I think he's rude, egotistical and overbearing."

Rowan's eyes danced as she unwrapped her sandwich. "Rude, eh? That's funny, because it seemed to me like he's totally into you."

Her words, so similar to what Henry had said, had my eyes shooting to hers. "Why would you think that?"

Rowan raised an eyebrow. "Well for starters he *watches* you. As in every move you make. He's not even being subtle."

"If he is watching me, Rowan," I said, "it's because he's suspicious of me. After what happened last night, that's only going to get worse."

"You think so?" Rowan asked, way too cheerfully, and took a bite of her sandwich.

"It's complicated." I sighed and fiddled with my soft drink. "Henry and I, well...we had a little *incident* at the office yesterday morning."

"*I knew it*!"

"We had a fight."

"You had sex." She pointed at me. "It's about time girl!"

My face went hot, and I dropped my head in my hands.

"Oh honey, was it bad?" All sympathy, Rowan patted my arm.

"It was okay. It's a little hard to explain."

"Tell me," she said.

So I swallowed my pride and told my cousin what

happened at the office, and how I'd bolted afterwards. She sat silently for a few moments.

"I feel like I got played, Rowan."

"You should thank your lucky stars he was considerate enough to use protection."

"But that meant he'd had them on hand—"

Rowan burst out laughing.

"Nearby," I corrected. "He had them *nearby*."

"Edmund," Rowan managed to get out between shrieks of laughter.

"Edmund?" I asked. "What the hell does Edmund have to do with anything?"

"I bet Edmund gave him a box of condoms as a house warming present," Rowan said.

"For goddess sake." I rubbed my forehead.

"Didn't he give you a box, after you first moved in here with Eli?" Rowan pointed out, "And told you to 'play safe'?"

"Shit," I remembered. "Yes. Yes, he did."

"I bet you still have them. You probably never even opened the box. My money says they're in your night stand drawer. My guess is Henry shoved *his* box in a desk drawer, and when you and he went after each other yesterday, he put them to use."

I tossed up my hands. "Whose side are you on?"

"Hannah, I'm on your side, always." Rowan's lips were trembling from holding back laughter. "I'm right though, aren't I? Still in the box in your nightstand?"

"Yeah." *Right next to that emerald ring that has me*

so confused and twisted up inside.

"Is the box still unopened?"

"Shut up." I glared at her.

Rowan smiled. "I saw you talking to Henry poolside yesterday after dinner. Did you two get into it again?"

"We did," I admitted, and gave her the details.

"Juicy!" Rowan said with a little sigh. "So, you stomp off, get a clairolfactory warning, and eventually catch an arsonist in the act." Rowan took a sip of soda. "How did Henry end up over there anyway?"

"I've been wondering that myself," I admitted. "I guess he followed me when I ran across the street."

"Hannah, he probably thought he was protecting you." Rowan tossed her braid over her shoulder. "The man has no idea how well you can protect yourself."

"Well, the bad news is, he probably does now."

"Eat your lunch." Rowan abruptly changed the topic, and pushed my untouched sandwich in front of me. "Afterwards I'm going to do your face and hair."

"Sweetie, I appreciate the offer, but I'm really not in the mood."

"You're going to change your mind." Rowan's eyes took on a topaz glow. "Because Henry Walker *will* be coming to see you tonight."

My stomach lurched at the thought of another confrontation. "You're sure?" I asked my cousin. "Tonight?"

"Yes, I'm sure." Rowan nodded. "So eat your lunch and then let me work my magick."

***

A floral delivery from Nathan and Ivy arrived right after Rowan left. The big vase of sunflowers and carnations were bright and cheerful, so I set them on the kitchen table where I could enjoy them. Grateful for the distraction, I called to thank them and spent a half hour convincing my younger brother that I was, indeed, okay.

Finally, Ivy yanked the phone away from him.

"Swear to goddess Pogue, I'll strike you mute if you don't stop haranguing your sister." I heard her tell my brother. "Hey there Wonder Woman," she said to me. "How are you feeling?"

I couldn't help but grin. "I'm feeling better. Thanks for the flowers."

"You're welcome. Hey, if you need anything, you call us. Okay?" Ivy said. "Anything at all."

"I will," I said and meant it. "Thanks, Ivy."

"Cool," she said. "Now I'd better let you go. Because you're about to have company."

"That's the second time today I've had someone tell me that."

"Yeah well, he's walking up the steps, right now. Talk to you later!" Ivy cheerfully said goodbye and hung up.

When the knock sounded on my door, I took a deep breath, and got up to check the spy hole. As was predicted, Henry Walker stood on the little landing, staring back at me almost as if he could see me through the door.

"Just a minute," I called out. I checked my appearance in the mirror. My hair fell in loose waves, and the makeup was fairly natural but with an edge. Rowan had also browbeat me into changing into a flattering lavender dress of soft jersey material. Suddenly very grateful I'd let Rowan work her mo-jo, I took a steadying breath and went to open the door. *Here we go,* I thought.

"Hannah," he said, and before I could react, he leaned in and dropped a quick hard kiss on my mouth.

Stunned, I didn't move a muscle. "Hello Henry," I said. Of all the ways I'd expected to be greeted, him planting one on me was *not* what I anticipated.

One corner of his mouth kicked up. "You look nice."

"Uh, thank you," I managed, and stepped back so he could enter. "Would you like to come in?" I asked politely.

He went straight to the couch "How's your leg?" he said. "Edmund told me you got some stitches." He patted the cushion next to him.

"It's sore, but I'm okay." I chose the overstuffed chair, wanting to keep some distance between us. There was something about him sitting in my house that had my stomach muscles clenching. The man's unpredictability made me nervous, and I didn't like that. Not at all. Going for casual, I sat down carefully to avoid hitting the back of my leg against anything. "How are you feeling?" I asked politely.

"Oh, I'm fine." He waved that question aside.

I nodded at his response, and watched as he made himself at home on my couch. He wore jeans as usual, and a kelly-green t-shirt that made his eyes a brighter shade of emerald. *I'd inherited a bewitched emerald, and Henry has emerald-green eyes.* I gulped over the thought.

"Darlin' we really need to talk about yesterday," he said.

I took a breath and tried to project serenity. "I already gave my statement to the police regarding the kid I saw setting the fire."

Henry leaned forward. "Are you psychic?" he asked bluntly.

I blinked at him. "Excuse me?"

"I overheard you and your sister yesterday."

"You were spying on us?"

"No." He shook his head. "I came inside and *accidentally* overheard you talking while you were on the stairs. But what I heard, explained a few things. After you took off running across the street, I decided to follow you."

I sat back in the chair and fought to keep my breathing slow and calm, while my mind raced. *If he thinks I'm merely a psychic, I could use that.* Even as I thought it, my stomach churned.

"Your sister never questioned it when you said you

smelled smoke and gasoline," he said. "Kayleigh told you to 'hone in' on it, and took it as gospel that you were right. She went straight to the phone and dialed 911."

"I'm thankful she did." I folded my hands in my lap. "They got there quickly enough to keep the fire from spreading across the yard to the Miller's house."

Henry wasn't smiling, but he appeared to be calm as he spoke. "That day Edmund asked you to consult on the robberies in the neighborhood? You told him you thought arson would likely be next. And it was. You knew that boy had a gun when those kids tried shoplifting at your folk's store—admitted to me later that you *smelled* it on him. Plus you tried to warn me yesterday that there would be an explosion."

"Too bad you didn't listen," I said dryly.

"So if I have this straight, Edmund uses you as a consultant because you're a psychic?"

I blew out a breath. "That's one way of looking at it."

"He flat out said to you that, 'he'd never known you to be wrong before when you put your *nose* to work on a case'."

"You really do have a penchant for eavesdropping," I said, keeping up my guard.

Henry smiled, and crossed his booted feet on the coffee table. "I did some research on the internet last night. Most of it was bullshit, but I came across a few interesting things."

"Oh?"

"There's this thing, where some psychics get their information by their sense of smell. *Clairolfaction*, they called it."

"Fascinating."

"Don't get all snooty with me Hannah, it turns me on."

My mouth dropped open. "What did you say to me?"

He sat, grinning at me. "There, that got your undivided attention."

I stood, and he rose to his feet as well. "Mr. Walker, I'm not sure what you hope to accomplish by questioning me this way—" Before I could finish my sentence, he had stepped around the trunk, wrapped a hand around my arm and tugged me to him. I landed with my hands trapped against his chest.

He smiled down in my face as I sputtered at him. "Warned you," he said in that gravelly voice. Unexpectedly, I got hit with a clairolfactory impression of patchouli and musk: *Desire.* The combination set off alarm bells in my head.

His hands slid up my back, and trapped in his eyes, I stood still while he gently, oh so gently, ran his fingers through my hair. He cupped the back of my head, and I had barely enough time to suck in a quick breath before he dipped me back and proceeded to kiss the brains right out of my head.

Now that's more like it! What was left of my mind shouted.

When he finally allowed me up for air he stayed close, studying my face. "Yesterday morning, during the storm, you should have told me it had been a while for you." Henry's quiet words had the blood rushing to my cheeks.

"I, ah..." I stammered.

"I would have been more careful if I would have known." He dropped his forehead to mine. "We rushed things a bit. *I* rushed things," he admitted. "I ought to have taken more care with you. I will next time."

I hadn't blushed so much since I was a teenager, and the fact that he could simultaneously embarrass me *and* make me want him totally pissed me off. "Next time?" I pulled away slightly. "What makes you think there will be a next time?"

He slid his hands down to my hips, pulled our bodies together, and simply held me. Caught off guard by the move, I started to shake.

Hannah," he whispered in my ear. "The fact that you're trembling, tells me there's going to be a next time."

"That's *anger* you're feeling," I said as he began to nibble on my ear. "I don't even like you. I happen to prefer nice men."

"Liar," he said, and moved his mouth to a spot between my neck and my shoulder that had my heart racing.

"I hardly know you." Despite myself, I ran my hands up his back, pulled him closer.

"We can fix that," Henry murmured, kissing his way down my neck.

I'm not sure what would have happened next, but the loud clatter of little feet on the steps had me flinching away from him. Henry stepped back as well, and the door slammed open as Eli made his typical dramatic entrance.

"Hi Mama! I'm home!" He flung himself at me as though it had been days instead of a few hours since he'd last seen me.

"Hi baby." I stooped over and hugged him.

"Hey, you're the pirate guy," Eli said, staring at Henry.

"This is Mr. Walker," I corrected. "You remember him."

"Call me Henry," he said to Eli.

"Hi." Eli smiled up at him and then switched to more important matters. "Mom I'm starving! What's for supper?" His backpack hit the floor, and his school papers almost made the table.

"Hey kid, do you like pizza?" Henry said before I could answer my son.

Eli's eyes lit up. "Can we have pepperoni pizza?"

"Sure, my treat," Henry said without asking me.

With a battle cry Eli was off to his bedroom. The cat came out from wherever he'd been napping and slunk past me to sit under the table.

"Eli," I called, "if you want pizza, you'd better come pick up your school papers and put your backpack away."

"Mom!" Eli complained as he bounced back in the room.

I sent Eli a look, and he pouted. "Fine," he announced, making the ultimate sacrifice of putting his things away.

I studied Henry who stood there grinning at Eli from ear to ear. "Henry," I began, "you don't have to take us out to eat."

"What's the matter, darlin'? Are you nervous?" Henry asked casually.

"What?" I said. "I am not." *Although, I was.*

Henry smiled. "I think it would be good for us to get to know each other better," he said over the ruckus of Eli running around. "You're the one who said you hardly knew me, so we'll get started working on that."

I frowned at him, feeling maneuvered.

"I find it hard to believe that the woman who broke an armed robber's nose with a broom handle, and who chases down arsonists would be skittish about going out with me for pizza."

"Skittish?" My back stiffened. "Hardly."

"Well then." Henry grinned at me. "It's all settled. We even have a chaperone."

***

Over the next few weeks Henry Walker and I got to know each other. We went to the movies, out to dinner, sometimes alone and sometimes with Eli. The dates were casual, and to my surprise Henry didn't press for more than a kiss goodnight. He made a comment to me that we'd taken things out of order, and I was a little caught off guard by a man who seemed more old fashioned. Especially considering how we'd started out.

Henry never asked me again about being psychic, and to my relief he didn't seem to remember anything about the fire, except following me into the Miller's backyard—and then waking up clear across it. He shrugged it off, blaming the lapse of memory on the mild concussion. I held my breath waiting for the other shoe to drop, and when he didn't bring it up again, I started to relax.

He took Eli and me out to the property he'd purchased. The old farmhouse needed work, but the barn and other structures on the property were in good shape. Eli ran around exploring the old house, and I realized as I listened to Henry talk about the future plans for the property that it wasn't hard to imagine him with a few horses, living out in the country.

At work he was fairly easy to get along with. He still didn't always return his calls, but he did maintain somewhat of a professional working relationship, and that relieved me. Edmund took the news of Henry and I seeing each other in stride, and he and Henry put in hours of surveillance and tracked down the arsonist who'd set the fire at the Miller's house. Once the teen was arrested, the burglaries in the Oak Hills neighborhood stopped. The local papers ran a story about the agency, and I was happy to stay in the background.

August rolled into September and still Henry hadn't made any moves towards the bedroom, and I could privately admit that it was starting to make me twitchy. The man could kiss, I'd give him that. I'd even taken him to my favorite beach and we'd walked through the surf alone, and had sat on the boulders making out like a couple of teenagers.

Afterwards I was convinced that he'd take me back to his apartment and we'd finally have sex, but to my shock he instead took me home, walked me to the door, ended the evening with another smoldering kiss, and left.

***

I parked behind the office and sat thinking about the past few weeks. Checking my reflection in the review mirror, I scowled. "If I didn't know any better I'd think the man was courting me, or something."

But that didn't make sense. Henry Walker wasn't a romantic. He was a schemer and a bit of a scoundrel. That's what I liked about him.

And honestly? I was starting to get suspicious. *What was he up to? What in the hell was he waiting for? Was he waiting for* me *to ask* him *to bed?* I blew out a frustrated breath, and admitted to myself that if the sexual tension between us wasn't relieved soon, I'd probably end up doing something drastic. However, considering how that had worked out the first and only time...it would probably be for the best if I let this play out.

I psyched myself up and strolled in to the office at a quarter to nine, trying to act casual. I smoothed my long black sundress down and went through my morning routine of booting up the computer and checking for voice mails. I was brewing myself a cup of tea when I caught a whiff of ocean, wind and beach.

Henry. I smiled.

He moved to my side and began to make himself a cup of coffee.

"Good morning," I said.

"We still have five minutes before official 'business hours'," he said, while he tucked a K cup in the machine.

I glanced up at the clock and sipped at my tea. "So we do."

He took the mug out of my hand, and caged me in by bracing his arms against the counter on either side of my hips. Henry leaned down and our lips had just met when—

"Morning!" Edmund sauntered into the kitchenette and smiled at the two of us.

The mood broken, I casually picked back up my tea. "If you'll excuse me, I need to go through the messages."

I found Henry standing over my desk a short time later. "Yes?" I asked.

"I was wondering," Henry said, handing me a file, "would you take a look at these and see if you pick up on anything?"

I glanced up and met his eyes. This was a big step for him, he knew it and so did I. He'd never, not once before, asked for my help with a case. Carefully, I accepted the file. "Are you asking me to consult?"

"Yes, I am. It's a runaway. He's fourteen years old, the cops don't have any leads, I'm running into dead ends, and his mother is scared. But I thought maybe you might be able to give me some new information."

"I'd be happy to," I said.

"I'll give you some space," Henry said. "Let me know if you get any information." He walked to his office.

I lifted a picture of the boy, a selfie printed from his own social media, and considered it. As I gazed at the photo, my nose began to tickle. I sneezed and had to grab a tissue. I caught the faintest whiff of something...but my eyes began to water and I sneezed again.

"Oh, man," I muttered. "I better not be coming down with a cold." I made a grab for the tissues on my desk and sneezed several more times, loud enough for Henry to come out and stare at me.

"Hannah." Edmund came out of his office too. "Did you forget to take your allergy medicine or something?"

Allergies, I thought it over. *The last time I'd had such an explosive reaction of sneezing was when I'd been around someone's longhaired golden retriever.* My fingers began to tingle where they rested on the files. "This is gonna sound weird," I wheezed, "but this kid is around dogs. A *lot* of dogs."

The expression on Henry's face went from concern to humor, and then to calculation. "Dogs, eh?" He dropped a kiss on my head and bolted out the door. "I have an idea."

"Well, well," Edmund said as soon as Henry had left. "Somebody's starting to come around to you being a consultant."

"We'll see," I rasped, and sipped at my tea.

Edmund slid the files off my desk, stepped back, and the sneezing and wheezing stopped as suddenly as it began. "Wow, that was weird," I said. "Even for me."

CHAPTER TEN

Henry didn't return to the office, but he'd texted me and let me know he'd found the runaway.

That cute nose of yours was dead on. He was hiding out behind a local kennel, in their supply shed.

I smiled and texted back: *The fee for my consulting service is: dinner.*

Come out to the farmhouse for dinner tonight. 6:00pm. Bring Eli. Was his reply.

I smiled over that, touched that he wanted to include Eli in the evening. I texted back, letting him know we'd be there and settled back in to my work.

That evening, I'd barely had the car off before Eli was letting himself out and running for the farmhouse "Henry, we're here!" Eli hollered, banging on the old screen door. I followed a bit more slowly, and caught Henry's grin as he opened the door.

"Hey little man." He ran a hand over Eli's head as he raced past. Henry stood waiting for me. He drew me in, kissed me, and we went straight back to the kitchen, where a pizza box rested on a card table.

Eli smelled pepperoni and cheered.

"The kitchen is starting to come back together," I said as we ate the pizza. "I love the deep blue cabinets that you went with, they're gorgeous."

"You ought to like them, you picked them out," Henry said.

"Well you needed more color in here with the white tile backsplash and gray countertops you chose," I said.

Eli had spotted the boxes the cabinets had arrived in, and as soon as dinner was finished he pulled the cardboard boxes into the adjoining living room and began to play.

"I'm glad you took out the wall between the kitchen and dining room," I told Henry as he used a box cutter to make a "door" and "windows" in the boxes for Eli. "This is going to be a great space to entertain in the future."

Henry tucked the utility knife in his pocket. "Hannah, step outside with me for a moment." He held out his hand, and I went to join him on the porch.

We sat side by side on the front steps as dragonflies chased each other across the grass. I took a deep breath and enjoyed the view. "It's nice to sit and listen to the quiet." I set my purse beside me and leaned against Henry's arm.

"Are you happy here?" Henry asked.

"It's great, all the fresh air and the breezes." Content, I leaned into him and relaxed.

"I keep waiting for you to open up to me," Henry began. "But I feel like you've been holding part of yourself back."

He was so solemn that my heart began to beat faster in my chest. "Is something wrong?" I asked him.

"I've been patient, giving you time to confide in me, on your own, but I think I deserve the truth from you."

"I'm not sure what you mean."

"I remember," Henry said, and those two little words terrified me.

"You remember what, exactly?" I struggled to remain calm.

"Everything."

"About?" I said with a half smile. *Don't react, don't react!*

"Don't sit there and pretend like you have no idea what I'm talking about."

"I—"

Henry tossed a quick peek over his shoulder, making sure Eli was still playing happily. "I *remember,* Hannah. I always have. I know what you did to me the day of the fire. I *saw* you."

I licked my lips against a mouth that had gone bone dry. "And what do you think you saw?"

His eyes were an angry glittering green as he sat next to me. "Fine." He clenched his jaw. "I saw you throw your hands out and the Miller's gate blew open. I was watching your face, when you sensed...smelled that the shed was going to explode."

Sitting beside him, I struggled against tears. "Go on," I said.

"You looked me in the eye, told me you were sorry, and made a motion with your hands..." He made a gesture similar to the magickal one I'd used on him. "Your eyes seemed to light up and the next thing I knew, something invisible hit me in the chest so hard that I was off my feet and shooting back through the air! I landed on my back in the grass—*yards* away from where I'd been standing."

I hugged myself, feeling suddenly cold while he spoke.

"I've been thinking about everything that's happened since I met you. Your psychic abilities, that day with the butterflies. Your cousin Rowan...I still can't figure out how she messed with my head like that." He stood and began to pace. "The way the door slammed shut at the spice shop—you made a similar hand gesture then too. I watched that surveillance video a thousand times. Somehow your hair and dress were rippling in the wind. And you were inside! That kid was horrified when he backed away from you, *and* he called you a Witch."

"What do you want from me, Henry?"

"How about a little honesty darlin'? Think you can you manage that?"

That did it. *Now, I was angry.*

"I don't owe you any explanations." I rose to my feet and we squared off. "If you could put your Southern pride and monumental male ego aside maybe you could admit that I *saved your life* the day of the fire."

"Tell me what is going on!" he snapped. "Just tell me the truth!"

"The truth is, very few people can handle anything that would be considered different, and because of that, we keep certain things to ourselves." I struggled as the element of air responded to me, as it did whenever I was very upset or angry. I saw with some alarm that storm clouds had begun to gather.

"*We?*" he zeroed in on that. "Are you talking about your family?"

"There are some things I can *not* discuss, Henry," I said very carefully, trying to pull my temper back from the edge. "Not even with you."

"Not even with someone who loves you?"

His words stunned me into silence. I opened my mouth, no sounds came out and I tried again. "You *love* me?" I finally managed to say, as the last of my control over my powers slipped away. The wind began to rise, and the dragonflies I'd admired earlier began to circle around me.

"For god sakes, Hannah!" He spun away in frustration and turned back. "Yes, I'm in love with you, damn it! And all you can say after everything, is that *you can't discuss it?*" Suddenly Henry froze in place and his eyes flared wide.

"What are you staring at?" I asked.

"There are dragonflies in your hair and on your shoulders," he whispered.

A jewel-bright hummingbird zipped between us, making Henry jerk back, and the man who had just professed to loving me gawked open mouthed and silent as more birds and dragonflies began to gather.

"Mama?" Eli's little face was pressed up against the screen door. He was crying.

"It's okay Eli," I said carefully. *He'd been watching us as we fought,* I realized, and my stomach rolled over.

Eli's bottom lip quivered. "Mama, I want to go home." He pushed the door open and ran to me.

Henry stood stock still and stared as the air between us filled with winged creatures. Bees, dragonflies, butterflies, birds...They swarmed around, landed on the porch railings, and on the steps. I shut my eyes and held my son. It was a defensive and foolish move. Because I knew when I opened my eyes again...I wouldn't like what I saw.

Henry Walker stood transfixed by the creatures of air that had descended. "What in the actual fuck..." Henry whispered, his face turning pale.

Silently, I leaned forward, grabbed my handbag and slung the strap over my shoulder, I picked up my son, and hitched him on my hip.

"Henry is scared, Mama," Eli whispered.

"I know, baby." With one hand I gestured and my heart broke a little. "Element of air," I said under my breath. "I call upon you. Please grant my request, distract him, and buy me a little time."

It worked. Henry didn't even see us anymore. His

eyes were too big in his face, and he was breathing far too quickly as the birds and insects gathered around him—creating a shield between us. I took a step back, and another, and still Henry didn't move. The glamour spell was holding. I walked away and got Eli into the car as quickly as I could.

"Bye, Henry," Eli whispered, and his forlorn words had me struggling against tears as I drove down the gravel lane, and out of Henry's life.

The magick started to slip, and I felt the impact in my chest as the spell ended. Above us the clouds went dark, and rain began to fall.

***

I called Edmund. I didn't know who else would really understand. My parents took Eli for the night, and Edmund arrived at my apartment within minutes. We sat on the couch, and he listened while I explained everything. "He told me he loved me," I sniffled. "I never expected that he felt that way…but after tonight, he'll never want to see me again."

"So you had to spell him after all." Edmund tucked me under his arm. "I'm sorry Hannah."

"After the spectacle the creatures of air put on, I had no other choice. I glamoured him, kept him focused on the show, so he wouldn't see us leave. His memories are probably still intact."

Edmund sighed. "Stubborn ass."

"Me or him?" I asked, and it came out all watery.

"Both of you." Edmund handed me a tissue. "Do you love him?"

"I was beginning to trust him, hoped he'd be satisfied thinking I was only a psychic. I thought maybe we might have a chance at a future." I sighed and rested my head on Edmund's broad shoulder. "But I was so busy trying to keep my magick hidden, and him distracted away from the truth, that I never realized he'd put the pieces together weeks ago."

"Oh, Hannah." Edmund shook his head.

"Henry's clever, so much more than I knew, and I'm the fool," I admitted.

Edmund pressed a kiss to my cheek. "And for you, protecting the legacy had to come first."

I wiped my eyes. "Yes."

"That Osborne-Pouge family vow of silence with outsiders is archaic," Edmund said. "It might have been necessary back in the day, or maybe a hundred years ago, but today, it's obsolete. No other families are nearly as secretive as yours."

"You think I like that it's this way?" I balled up the tissue in my hand. "I'd do anything to change it."

"Maybe you need to reevaluate what keeping this vow has cost you," Edmund said. "Trying to keep your Witchcraft a secret from Henry might have ruined any chance of a relationship you could have built with him."

"I can't ignore over three hundred years of my family's tradition and practices," I reminded him.

"I'm not saying you should ignore it," Edmund argued. "I'm encouraging you instead, to be the one who *revolutionizes* it."

The front door opened and to my surprise, Henry walked right in. I squeaked in surprise and started to sit up from where I'd been curled in Edmund's arms.

Edmund tightened his grip and kept me where I was.

Henry glared. "You're damn lucky that you're my best friend, Edmund."

"Back at you," Edmund said, "because if you weren't one of my oldest friends, I'd punch you for making my best girl cry."

"Hannah and I need to talk," Henry addressed Edmund.

"No we really don't," I muttered.

"Yes, you really do." Edmund shifted and rose to his feet. "I'll be right outside," he said to both of us. "If I hear anything I shouldn't, I'm coming back in here."

"I didn't come here to fight with you," Henry said directly to me, in a quiet tone that had my hackles rising.

Edmund stopped at the door. "Remember what I said, Hannah. Be the one who begins a revolution." He winked at me and shut the door behind him.

Henry remained standing, and I stayed where I was, sitting at the far end of the couch.

"Where's Eli?" Henry asked. "He was crying when you left, is he okay?"

How was I supposed to keep my heart protected

when the man asked about my son—before anything else? "He's over with my parent's. He's okay."

"May I sit down?" Henry asked formally.

"I guess." My mind was whirling.

This polite, cautious Henry was a stranger to me. I was used to the Southern scoundrel, with the underhanded charm. I was much more comfortable with that side of his personality. I clasped my hands in my lap and stared at the floor as I tried to work out how to begin, and what to say first.

He sat on the opposite side of the couch. "After everything that happened today, the least you could do is look at me."

I steadied myself and met his eyes. The silence stretched for a good minute as we waited to see who would speak first.

"You disappeared," Henry finally said. "You took Eli and left. I told you that I loved you, and you ran from me. Why would you do that?"

"When we argued I thought it best to leave. Eli was upset, I was losing control of my temper, and you were afraid." I exhaled. "Of me."

"I wasn't afraid of you."

"You were wide eyed, pale and shaking," I argued. "You *were* afraid."

"Stunned maybe," Henry corrected.

"Henry, there was a time when that sort of reaction would have caused people like me to be hunted down, drowned, hanged or even burned at the stake..." I trailed off, struggling to continue.

"It's okay." Henry's eyes were intense as he leaned forward. "You can trust me."

I shifted my body on the couch, made eye contact and took a leap of faith. "In my family, Henry, there's a tradition. A legacy, and one we've kept closely guarded for over three hundred and twenty-five years. With this comes certain gifts, and those gifts carry very specific obligations."

"Such as silence with outsiders."

"Correct." I nodded. "The tradition of silence is one that, to my knowledge, had never been broken with an outsider, until today."

"I understand." Henry reached for my hand. Held it.

"No I really don't think that you do." I slid my hand away. "We're *different*, and not everyone can handle that. Seeing your reaction today broke my heart."

"Maybe you could cut me a break, Hannah," Henry said. "You can't expect a man not to have a reaction when you whip out a display like that."

"Display?" Despite myself, I was offended.

"Element of air, right?" Henry pointed at me. "Darlin' you put on one hell of a show. Ticked all the boxes, called all the...hang on," he trailed off and snapped his fingers. "Ah, I got it now. Associated creatures that relate to the element."

He'd stated that information so casually. All I could do was stare at him.

"Nothing to say?" He crossed his arms, waited.

"I'm simply surprised at your level of information," I said.

"Well I figure if a man gets involved with a Witch, then he damn well better hit the books and study."

"You've been studying?" I raised my eyebrows.

"Sure, I've been reading all sorts of books. Got a bunch of them at my apartment. Edmund even recommended a few."

My mouth hit the floor. "Edmund?"

"Well, yeah he saw the first book I bought, threw it in the garbage and hauled me down to a metaphysical shop and loaded me up with better books."

"Edmund, took you shopping for books on the occult?"

"Yeah he did. I drew the line at going shopping for clothes with him—he claimed I needed a new wardrobe...but anyway, I've learned quite a bit, actually."

"I can't tell you how very reassuring that is to me." I sniffed.

"You go right on talking all snooty like that—it gives me hope." Henry grinned. "Besides, you know what it does to me."

"This is hardly the time to make jokes, Henry."

"I'm not trying to make light of your legacy, as you call it. Not at all. I love you Hannah, I meant what I said. You can trust me."

My heart began to speed up. *Was it possible? Did I get to have the faery tale after all?* "I do trust you." I smiled.

"Thank you," Henry said as he pulled me close, and held me.

I cuddled up against him. "I didn't think you'd accept me, few people could."

"It drove me crazy that you wouldn't trust me with your secret." He pressed a kiss to the top of my head. "Made me worry you didn't think I was worthy of you."

"I was afraid to let you get too close, but you did anyway."

"I'm sneaky that-a-way," Henry drawled.

"Yes, you are." I waited a moment. "You're absolutely sure that you can handle this? Very few mundane people can adjust to the reality of magick in their lives."

"Well, life certainly won't be boring." Henry grinned. "I am as serious as you are about this. I love you, Hannah. That's not going to change."

"Can I ask you something?" I said quietly.

"Sure."

"Why haven't you made love to me since that first time? What are you waiting for?"

Henry tipped my chin up. "I'm waiting for you to tell me that you're ready."

My stomach did a quick backflip. "And if I told you I was ready, right now?"

His eyes narrowed. "Is Eli coming back tonight?"

"No," I said. "He's staying with my parents."

"Do you have a lock on your bedroom door, just in case?"

I nodded. "Yes, there's a lock on the door."

Henry stood up and held out his hand. Silently I took it. Without a word we walked across the floor to my bedroom and stepped inside.

The room was softly lit from the little lamp on the night stand, and the windows were open, as I preferred them. A soft breeze ruffled the sheer curtains allowing the sounds and scents of the nighttime gardens into the room. I swallowed past the lump in my throat, shut the door and locked it.

Henry dropped his hands on my shoulders and I leaned back into him. He ran his hands down and over my body, and slowly turned me to face him. We stared into each other's eyes for a long moment. This time there wouldn't be any hurried coupling in the dark. This time would be completely different.

Suddenly more nervous than I cared to admit, I jolted when he ran a hand along the side of my face. "Don't be afraid," he whispered in that gruff voice.

I managed to smile. "I'm not." Now that the moment of truth had arrived, I was more nervous as to Henry seeing my body in the light. I'd had a child, and was full figured. My body wasn't perfect like some underwear model.

He pulled his t-shirt over his head, and my inner ramblings skidded to a halt. For the first time I saw his naked chest. I was so distracted at the play of muscles that it took me a moment to notice the tattoo on his right shoulder.

It was a Jolly Roger.

"You have a pirate flag tattoo," I managed to say.

"Yeah," Henry said. "Something wrong?"

As I focused on the design, everything around me seemed to slow down, and my heartbeat sounded loud to my own ears. His tattoo *was* all done in black, and I ran my fingers over the ragged flag that appeared to ripple and featured a skull with two crossed swords beneath.

Watch for the Pirate, Hannah, my grandmother's voice whispered through my memories and it had me blinking tears from my eyes. I started to smile as everything at last clicked into place.

"Well there you are." I smiled up at him. "I've been watching and waiting for you."

"I've been waiting for you, too," he said.

We reached for each other, and our kiss was explosive. My dress quickly went the way of his shirt, and he reached around behind me to unclasp my bra. He tugged the pink lace bra free and my breasts dropped heavily down.

"Finally," he said, bending to lavish kisses across them. I held his head as he drew one peak into his mouth and began to suckle.

And here I'd worried that maybe my breasts were too big, I thought. But by the praises he was whispering across them, clearly Henry didn't think so. He stood abruptly and in a few short steps we were both easing down on the bed. He nudged me back and tugged my underwear down my legs. I waited and watched as he unbuttoned and unzipped, allowing his pants to drop.

Now that I had a clear look at him, I began to understand why our first time together had been difficult. "You're gorgeous," I breathed as he stood there in front of me.

He grinned at that, and I steadied my voice and told him where I had the condoms. He nodded and reached into the drawer. Hearing him tear the box open had me shuddering in anticipation. I gulped as he rolled one on and slowly crawled over to me. He pulled me up and we knelt on the bed. He dropped a kiss on my shoulder, turned me in his arms, and the strongest sense of déjà vu swept over me as I relived the first vision the poesy ring had ever given me.

The light was misty, the sound was muffled and the air was heavy and expectant. Henry's strong muscular arms wrapped around me from behind, holding me firmly but gently, and I gasped from my need of him.

He dropped kisses in the spot between my shoulder and neck, and feeling his whiskers rub across my skin as I'd once experienced from the vision made me shiver. He murmured in my ear, asking if I was ready for him, and tested for himself with gentle fingers. He sounded satisfied by what he'd found, and his touch had my heart racing and muscles clenching in reaction.

"*Yes*," I whispered.

Henry gently arranged me to his liking. I was held in place by one of his hands on my hip, and the other that was tangled in my hair. He slid in slowly, and carefully, a little at a time. I threw my head back, panting and tried to push back, wanting to feel *all* of him.

"Easy," he warned.

The sensations were overwhelming. When he finally slid in to the hilt, I could have sworn I felt him bump against my cervix. "By the goddess," I moaned, as he held me in place giving my body time to adjust to his invasion.

My hands gripped the quilt covering the bed as Henry wrapped his arms across my breasts. He pulled me up so that my back was tight against his chest. Finally he began to move. Slowly and deliberately at first, and then stronger and faster.

He filled me up with long, sure strokes that had me shuddering with pleasure. When he reached down and touched that little bundle of nerves, I bit my lip against crying out at the amazing sensations.

I was close...so close to the orgasm of my life. I tried to hold out, and make it last longer but the sensations were too much. When it crashed over me I surrendered to it, and the waves of pleasure rolled over, taking the both of us.

I came back down to earth and discovered that I was sprawled on my belly with my head dangling off the side of the bed. Henry was right next to me, with one hand on my butt, and his whiskers tickling my shoulder.

I gasped when his hand gave my backside a playful smack. "Hey," I grumbled, twisting my head to glare at him.

"You finally awake?" He grinned at me.

I shook my head and scooted back so I was fully on the mattress. "I am now." I snuggled closer, and sighed happily.

I indulged myself by running my hands over his naked chest. He allowed it for a while, and to my surprise the man moved down, and with one hard tug, looped my knees over his shoulders. He began kissing the insides of my thighs and I sank my hands in his hair.

"Helping yourself, are you?" I asked giving his tousled curls a yank.

He smirked up at me, his mouth hovering right above my most sensitive area. "Want me to stop?" He flicked his tongue over me, and I bit back a scream.

"Don't you dare stop," I said on a breathless laugh.

CHAPTER ELEVEN

I'd never had someone make love to me all night long before. *It was wonderful.* He allowed me a few naps between rounds, but by the time the sun came up, I was feeling very relaxed. I had to keep myself from grinning like a lunatic as I got up, got dressed, and started breakfast.

Eli came home and burst through the door. He started to run straight to me and skidded to a stop when he saw Henry sipping coffee in the kitchen. "Are you and Mama still fighting?" he asked him.

I started to answer, but Henry sent me a look. "No we aren't," he said to Eli. "I love your Mama, and I'm sorry you saw us argue yesterday."

Eli seemed to think that over. "I fight with Margot sometimes. Mama always makes me 'pologize."

I held my hand out to Eli. He came and took it. "Eli—"

"Did you 'pologize to Henry?" he interrupted.

"Yes, I apologized." I kissed the top of Eli's head.

"And I apologized too," Henry said.

Eli tugged on my hand. "You scared him with the rutabaga mom. We're not supposed to do that."

"You're right, I messed up. I'm sorry Eli."

"Rutabaga?" Henry started to chuckle. "One of y'all want to fill me in on that?"

"It's a code word for *magick*," I explained. "It's what my father taught us when we were little."

While I got our breakfast ready, Henry set the table with some assistance from Eli, and I listened, amused, as my four year old brought Henry up to speed on the family rules—as he understood them—regarding magick.

To his credit, Henry listened carefully, and watching them together had my heart aching in the best possible way. The reality of it hit me suddenly and like a ton of bricks. *I was in love with Henry Walker.* My knees wobbled, but I managed to hold it together.

"So is Henry going to stay with us now?" Eli asked as he finished up his scrambled eggs. "He could sleep in my room."

"Maybe," Henry answered before I could. "Or maybe someday you and your Mama will come out and live with me at the farmhouse."

My breath caught, and the piece of toast I'd been buttering slipped out of my hand and plopped on my plate. "Henry?"

"Well honey, I didn't have you out at the farmhouse all those times because I needed decorating advice,"

Henry said. "For a woman who's supposed to be a psychic, you sure didn't get that I was remodeling the place with you and Eli in mind."

"We'd live at your house?" Eli's eyes were very large as he stared up at Henry. "Like a family?"

"I sure hope so." Henry ran his hand over Eli's bright hair. "I'd be honored if you'd be my family."

Henry's words had happy tears rolling down my face, and before I could say anything, Eli was out of his chair and diving in Henry's lap for an enthusiastic hug. "I knew it! Captain Time promised me that you'd be my new dad."

"Who's Captain Time?" Henry asked.

"Captain Timmons," I corrected. "I'll explain it to you later."

***

Later that night, Henry and I lay in my bed, talking quietly. I explained to him about the poesy ring I'd inherited, and how my grandmother had predicted his arrival, Eli's imaginary friend, who was probably the ghost of an ancestor, and—without going into *graphic* detail, I told him a little about the visions I'd had of a mystery lover with a pirate flag tattoo.

Henry started to chuckle. "So that's why you're so fascinated by the tattoo."

"Bewitched, more like." I ran my hands across his chest, and lower, smiling when he shuddered in reaction at my explorations. I reached over to kiss him and he rolled me underneath, pinning my hips with his.

I felt him reach across the bed, and I started to laugh when I heard him yank the drawer completely out of the nightstand. It fell to the floor with a racket, and I held my breath waiting to see if Eli would wake up.

"Give me a minute." Henry rolled out of bed, grabbed the contents from the floor, and dumped them on top the night stand. He padded over, locked the bedroom door, and came back to me with a smile.

"Where were we?" I asked as I slid my hands up his chest.

"Right about here," he said.

I was nipping at the side of his neck, and he pulled my legs up higher. I gasped as he slid inside me, his thrusts slow and deep. In response, I wrapped my arms and legs around him and hung on.

As the final vision from the poesy ring played out in real time, a sense of happiness and peace filled me up. I struggled against tears and shuddered at the words I knew were about to be spoken.

Henry tangled his hands in my hair. "Damn it, I love you," he growled.

His words thrilled me. "I love you too," I whispered, kissing my way down his neck, and across the tattoo that was on his upper right shoulder.

My admission spurned him on and I hung on and enjoyed the wild ride.

Afterwards we lay in the dark; sweaty, out of breath,

and in each others arms.

"Took you long enough to say it," Henry sighed.

"I didn't know for sure until today," I admitted. "But when you sat talking with Eli in the kitchen about the 'rutabaga rule', that's when I knew you were the one for me." I rolled over on top of him and dropped a kiss on his smart mouth. "I certainly never thought I'd fall for a scoundrel, with a slow, Southern accent and a cocky attitude."

"I knew you would," Henry said smugly. "Fall for me, that is. I'm a pretty charming guy after all."

"It's a shame you don't have more self-confidence, Mr. Walker." I raised my eyebrows and propped myself up on his chest.

"You're just trying to turn me on again, talking like that."

"Is it working?" Out of the corner of my eye I saw a bright green glow.

"What's that light?" Henry asked and reached for the carved box that was out on the nightstand.

"Be careful with that," I warned as he sat up.

"Is this the poesy ring you told me about?" Henry flipped the lid up but didn't touch the jewel.

"It is. Christopher Timmons first gave that to his bride—my ancestor, Felicity."

Henry whistled in appreciation at the jewel. "So the emerald is glowing. That's a good thing, right?"

I leaned over his shoulder to see for myself. The stone practically pulsed, shining in a vibrant tone of the clearest of deep greens. "Yes, it's a very good thing." I reached over, and carefully closed the lid. A faint green glow continued to seep out from around the edges of the box.

"Tell me what that glow is supposed to mean again?" he asked.

I placed the carved wooden box back on the nightstand. "Think of it as a confirmation and a blessing."

"That's got me to thinking..." Henry trailed off.

"Yes?" I asked and lay back down with him.

"Instead of a diamond, maybe I should buy you an emerald. A smaller one, mind you...Since an emerald helped us find our way together, that seems like the only logical choice for an engagement ring."

I hid a smile at his self-confidence. "Well then, I would honestly prefer something smaller, as you said. It'd be much more wearable."

Henry pressed a kiss to my mouth. "Deal," he said.

I swore I felt my heart skip a beat. "*If* we ever get to that point—"

"When," Henry said. "I'll want to speak to your father first."

"Seriously?" I gaped at him. "What century are we in?"

Henry laughed. "Well I'm not sure how all this works with Witches. Are there any marriage rituals I should know about?"

"Handfasting," I corrected. "Didn't you come across

any in your books?"

"Hmmm, I think I remember seeing something about that." Henry leaned down and kissed me. "But I have to tell you, I was a little disappointed that I didn't find any mating rituals."

I snorted out a laugh. "You sure you're up for that, Walker?"

He pulled my arms over my head, pinned my hands with one of his, and smiled. "Try me." His voice was a challenging sort of purr.

As the light of a waxing moon filtered through the windows, the stars sparkled and the breeze carried a hint of the sea inside. Henry and I laughed, loved again and made plans for our future together as a family of three.

My legacy wasn't hidden any longer, but the poesy ring had given us its blessing. We'd become bewitched and beloved, and blessed by the moon, stars, and sea.

The End

The Legacy Of Magick series continues with, *Spells of The Heart.*
Available now!